"I thought maybe ... imagined ..." Logan said

"Imagined...?" Lily's jacket was unzipped to her breastbone, with only a thermal silk undershirt beneath.

"This." With a light touch he put his bare finger to the pulse racing at the base of her throat.

All she could hear was the thump, thump, thumping of her heart beating too fast in her ears. Her clothes felt too tight—or maybe that was her own skin. A heavy anticipation filled the cold air and she tried to tell herself it was something she'd felt often. Had acted on often.

But today, with this man, it felt startlingly, shockingly different.

She took some comfort in the fact his own pulse, beating at his throat, was no steadier than hers. "This...what?" she asked.

Something flashed in his eyes. "I'm not sure I can put it into words without being graphic."

Her body let out a shiver and, honest to God, her knees wobbled. "I see."

He leaned so close that visions of them ripping off each other's clothes danced in her head and all she wanted was his mouth to touch hers. "So, what are we going to do about...this?"

Dear Reader,

The mountain and ski lodge in *Free Fall* is fictitious, but it's a setting near and dear to my heart. I wrote this story during the summer, and every time I described the snow and the skiing, I yearned for winter and to be back out on the slopes! So I hope I made it come alive for you.

This is my last Harlequin Temptation novel, and I'll miss the line so much! Look for me in the Harlequin Blaze line if you get a chance. In the meantime, hope you enjoy *Free Fall*, and happy reading.

Jill Shalvis

Books by Jill Shalvis

HARLEQUIN TEMPTATION

845—AFTERSHOCK
861—A PRINCE OF A GUY
878—HER PERFECT STRANGER
885—FOR THE LOVE OF NICK
910—ROUGHING IT WITH RYAN*
914—TANGLING WITH TY*
918—MESSING WITH MAC*
938—LUKE
962—BACK IN THE BEDROOM
995—SEDUCE ME

HARLEQUIN BLAZE

63—NAUGHTY BUT NICE
132—BARED

HARLEQUIN FLIPSIDE

5—NATURAL BLOND INSTINCTS

HARLEQUIN SINGLE TITLE

THE STREET WHERE SHE LIVES

*South Village Singles

JILL SHALVIS

FREE FALL

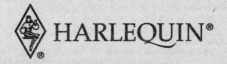

HARLEQUIN®

TORONTO • NEW YORK • LONDON
AMSTERDAM • PARIS • SYDNEY • HAMBURG
STOCKHOLM • ATHENS • TOKYO • MILAN • MADRID
PRAGUE • WARSAW • BUDAPEST • AUCKLAND

ISBN 0-373-69215-3

FREE FALL

This edition published by arrangement with Harlequin Books S.A.

® and TM are trademarks of the publisher. Trademarks indicated with
® are registered in the United States Patent and Trademark Office, the
Canadian Trade Marks Office and in other countries.

www.eHarlequin.com

Printed in U.S.A.

Prologue

Denton, Ohio

"SO WHICH ONE OF YOU SEXY hotshots is the best man?"

Search-and-rescue expert Logan White looked up in surprise as his entire team pointed to him.

The nurse asking the question flashed him a hundred-watt smile. "You? Well, then, sugar, it's your lucky night." And she ripped the light blue scrubs right off her body.

Logan, a man who'd seen and done it all and who'd thought himself unshockable, nearly swallowed his tongue. Beneath the scrubs, the nurse wore a cherry-red thong with matching pasties strategically placed over her nipples.

His best friend, Wyatt Stone—the reason for the bachelor party going on around them—grinned at him. "A little something from me to you, man. Thanks for being the greatest best man and best friend a guy could ask for." He hoisted his beer in a toast as their friends, normally as serious and intense as their profession demanded, laughed and hooted and hollered like a group of frat boys on spring break.

Just last night the lot of them had been rappelling

down the side of a mountain in a vicious rainstorm, searching for a lost teen who'd gotten separated from her hiking group. Logan had flown the mission, and when the winds had kicked up, things had gotten so tense, so damned dangerous in the ravines above the river on a black, black night, that he'd been only half convinced he could help them all out to safety.

Now they sat in the swank private suite of a downtown hotel, surrounded by posh, elegant furniture and a fully stocked bar with the large-screen TV playing the latest basketball game, acting like a pack of dogs, howling at the three nurses who'd come into the room looking for someone to "make feel better." It was hard to reconcile, especially since he'd been working so hard he could barely remember what it was like to just breathe.

Logan had expected the strippers—hell, he'd helped pay for them. But the women in hospital scrubs—a uniform he saw daily—had thrown him off. The now nearly naked bleached blonde smiled when her two accomplices, also stripping out of their uniforms, hit Play on their portable CD player. Loud, pulsing dance music filled the air.

The woman standing in front of Logan began to move to the beat. She was twenty-one, maybe twenty-two, making him feel ancient at thirty-one, and he turned to Wyatt. "She should be dancing for you— *Oof.*"

Teetering in her red five-inch stilettos, she plopped herself in his lap. With a shrieking laugh, she straddled his thighs, hers wide open as she wriggled and squirmed, writhing and arching to the thumping music, grinding her crotch to his, eventually getting the sought-for reaction from him, albeit a purely physical one.

Her arms encircled his neck as she thrust her large, expensive-looking breasts in his face. "Ready for your present, best man?"

"Uh—"

She wriggled some more, and the corner of a small envelope peeked out from the front of her thong. "Just for you," she purred, continuing to shimmy and shake. Her breasts threatened to give him a black eye. "Take the prize, hot stuff."

With a wince—*hot stuff?*—he pulled the envelope out of her thong and discovered she wasn't a bleached blonde but the real thing. And then felt like a pervert.

It was a relief to focus on tearing open the envelope. The card inside was a certificate for a seven-night stay at a Lake Tahoe resort. Logan just stared at it. Sure, he loved to ski, but he didn't feel the need to go away. Why would he, when he did and saw things on a daily basis that most other people wouldn't even dream of: climbing mountains, flying helicopters and rappelling out of them. Lake Tahoe couldn't possibly dish up anything to compare.

"Wyatt, this is too much. You and Leah should use this yourselves—"

"Oh, no. We're off to a warmer climate, thank you very much, where little to no clothing is required. This Tahoe trip is yours, buddy, for all you've done for me."

He was referring to how Logan had saved his life,

and Leah's, as well, only a few months back. But Logan didn't want to be paid for that. That was what he did. It was who he was.

The stripper in his lap was still working the beat, and he gently set her off him. "I don't need a week off. I don't *have* a week off."

"What are you talking about?" Wyatt laughed. "We work for ourselves. You want a week, you take a week."

Yes, they worked for themselves. Mostly. He and Wyatt co-owned the helicopter he'd flown last night. They supported their joint helicopter habit with paying jobs—Wyatt flew for the local TV and radio stations, and Logan flew a couple of local millionaires around at their whim during their business day. But they also worked volunteer for the SAR team, both men living for and loving the times they were called to fly search and rescue.

"It's not that simple," he protested now. "I have jobs scheduled, and with you going on your honeymoon, I'll need to be available to fly for SAR 24/7."

"So wait until I get back. But you're going. You need to get away, every bit as much as I do." Their eyes met, and all the things they'd done and seen shimmered between them.

The stripper Logan had set aside shifted her attention to Wyatt, who sat back, easygoing and smiling at her slow, sensuous movements. But Logan knew his partner extremely well. Wyatt's thoughts were elsewhere. Probably with Leah, who he'd be marrying tomorrow.

Marrying. Logan shuddered. He had no idea why in the world Wyatt would want to screw up a good relationship with marriage.

He watched his old friend draw the stripper's attention away from himself and onto two of their oldest buddies, who eagerly lapped up everything she dished out, and he had to admit that if any couple could make it in the crazy, dangerous world he and these guys all lived in, Wyatt and Leah could. They had a rare, beautiful, deep connection—one Logan had never really experienced himself.

"Maybe you'll meet a hot ski bunny," Wyatt said, and waggled his eyebrows.

"A hot ski bunny." Logan had to laugh. "Is that what you think I need?"

"You need something, starting with a week off. Take the trip," Wyatt said quietly. "I have a feeling about it."

"A feeling? Hell. You fall like a brick for a woman and now you're thinking like one."

"Okay, how about this—you worked every single day last month, and I think the month before that, too. If you haven't been at the mercy of a Trump wannabe, you've been risking life and limb for perfect strangers. It's a bad equation that equals burnout."

Logan looked at the strippers, and—unmoved by their gyrations—he admitted that Wyatt had a point. Burnout *was* lurking, flickering at the edges of his mind. He needed to get away, and skiing his brains out on Wyatt's dime sounded…good. Damn good. "Fine, but if you have to come drag me back, it's your own fault."

"Duly noted, man. Duly noted. Just make sure to cut loose and have fun."

Yeah. Logan figured if he really tried, he might manage to do just that.

1

Lake Tahoe, California

"LILY ROSE? YOU KNOW IT'S payday, right?"

Oh, for God's sake. Lily Harmon's head was going to blow right off her shoulders. Truly. If she didn't get a moment of peace in her immediate future, she couldn't be held responsible for what came next.

Knowing that, and her own limited patience, she drew a deep, calming breath, turned away from her ski locker and smiled blankly at her older sister, Gwyneth. "Really? It's payday?"

Gwyneth's mouth fell open. "You *did* forget."

"Nah. I just like watching you grow gray hair before my eyes."

Gwyneth was thirty-five to Lily's twenty-five, and not a single day went by that she didn't fling around the extra wisdom that those ten years supposedly granted her. "I was just trying to help."

"You can save your breath." Lily dug back into her locker. "I have the general manager job down."

"But—"

"Look, if you feel the need to waste some of your own time, go find someone else to waste it on. And, sheesh, while you're at it, try to relax a little." Lily pulled her red ski-patrol jacket over her head, then buckled on the small fanny pack that held all her essentials—not a brush or lip gloss or anything that Gwyneth's pack might have contained, but a first-aid kit, a screwdriver for fixing bindings and other various handy items.

"How about the statistic reports?" Gwyneth said. "Did you get my memo—" She broke off at the look of steel in Lily's eyes. "Right. You're fine."

"You know what you need instead of that anal accounting job, Gwynnie? Someone to boss around. Have some kids. Then you can bicker with them all day and turn into Mom." Lily jammed on her helmet and eyed her snowboard and skis. *Board*, she decided. She stomped into her boots and snatched the board, and then glanced at Gwyneth, who was still standing there looking like the substitute teacher whose class had all ditched on her.

Shaking her head, Lily walked out of the ski-locker area and into the open lodge, where a handful of guests milled around in various stages of ski-gear dress. She moved past the huge stone fireplace where the roaring fire she herself had started at the crack of dawn this morning was still going strong. The comfy chairs and sofas in deep, inviting colors, strategically placed to capture the warmth of the flames, were filled with guests; some talking, laughing, some taking in the ambience of the cabin walls that were dotted with photos from the lodge's past hundred years.

The scene always brought a smile to her face—a smile that faded when she realized that Gwyneth had caught up with her and was back to checking off items on her ever-present clipboard. "We're having bear problems in the trash again."

"What? After you authorized the purchase of the correct boxes with the suggested latches that the bears can't get into?" Lily silently predicted that her sister would miss the sarcasm.

"Yes, but now the bears aren't the only ones who can't get into the trash. Our guests can't, either, and they don't understand that we actually get a lot of bears waking up all winter long. So now the bears are simply hanging out by the bins, waiting for the guests to leave the trash on the ground beside the bins."

Yep. No sense of humor at all. "I've already ordered more Do Not Feed The Bears Or Else Lose Your Life signs, along with better directions for getting into the trash bins. It's not rocket science, so I'm sure our guests will figure it out with the help of the extra pictures."

Gwyneth's mouth tightened. "Also, it's end of month. The payables and receivables need to be—"

"Right. I've got a calendar."

"Okay, but also there's the—"

"Good Lord." Lily tipped her head back to take in the huge wood beams running the length of the large lodge that she'd been walking through all of her life. Then she turned to her sister. "Look at me, Gwyneth. Do I look like I give a crap that you're chasing after me and listing all my responsibilities, as if I was a five-year-old?"

Gwyneth's lips all but disappeared now. "No. No, you don't."

"Good. So maybe *you* could try not to give a crap if once in a while I do things my way. What do you think?"

Gwyneth slowly let the clipboard down to her side. "I'm not trying to nag. I just want to see Bay Moon under control."

Bay Moon Resort was a big, fancy name for a place that wasn't really big or fancy but just right. They had fifteen guest rooms, a full-service cafeteria, a bar, a gift shop and a ski-rental shop. They also had a reputation for being one hell of a gathering spot, attracting so many repeat visitors on their mountain and in their lodge every year that getting into the place had become tough enough for the Lake Tahoe brochures to give them the coveted "exclusive" title.

Lily didn't think of the place as exclusive so much as…home. Gwyneth didn't feel the same way, nor did their middle sister, Sara. That's because Gwyneth and Sara had lived with their parents in town while Lily, the problem child, had been sent here after a series of "unfortunate incidents" involving some admittedly bad choices on her part. She'd come to Grandma and Grandpa's resort at age sixteen, as slave labor for "straightening out."

And boy howdy, how she'd gotten straightened out. It hadn't been her grandpa's lightning temper or her grandma's lectures, either, though both had probably contributed. It had been the mountain itself that gave her a sense of peace and the strength to just be herself. "Bay Moon *is* completely under control." She stopped before the huge double wooden doors that would lead her into the glorious Sierra winter and right to the ski lifts that were her own personal wonderland. Before she'd even graduated high school, she'd been an emergency medical technician and certified professional ski patroller—nothing but a disguise on her part, really, one that had allowed her to work as ski patrol on the slopes she loved with all her heart.

Until she'd been given the general manager position.

She was still an EMT, still a certified patroller, only now things were different, more complicated, and she didn't get out as often as she'd like. In fact, she hardly got out at all.

"Lily Rose, I'm trying to talk to you."

"No, you're trying to drive me crazy." She pressed her temples to keep her brains from exploding. "And you're doing a fine job, too. I'm asking you to back off."

"How can I do that? If I didn't stand on top of you, you wouldn't get anything done."

Lily gaped at that. Gwyneth still, after all this time, truly believed it was the nagging that made Lily tick. She could tear her hair out over that, but the truth was, there had been a time when she'd have needed someone on top of her. She'd sneaked out regularly. She'd pulled pranks, such as running the snowmaking machines in July or filling the water tap in the cafeteria with green food coloring, freaking out guests and employees alike. She'd even stolen a vehicle—if you could call it *stealing* to borrow a snowcat to go four-wheeling beneath a midnight moon...

She'd been a handful, no doubt, but damn it, she'd paid the price. Her family never looked at her and saw a grown-up—even now, they still saw her as that wild child.

She could deal with that. She *was* dealing with that. "You know I've been running this place since Grandma died last year, and without any major snafus."

Gwyneth crossed her arms. "You say that as though you've never screwed up."

"Right." Lily had to laugh. "How could I deny it when we both know you remember each and every long-ago transgression?"

Gwyneth sighed. "This isn't about your past. Wild or otherwise."

The hell it wasn't. But she absolutely didn't want to get her sister going on the subject because it usually took Gwyneth a good long time to list every single indiscretion of Lily's errant youth. Far too long to be standing still on a rocking January morning when a foot of fresh powder was calling her name. "Tell you what. Let's call a truce."

"A truce?"

"Yes. I'm sorry Grandma left Bay Moon to me and not you, and you're sorry you're uptight and anal."

"But you're not sorry Grandma left Bay Moon to you when she died last year."

"Okay, you caught me." She smiled, but Gwyneth did not, making her sigh. "Look, this place is small and perfect the way it is, and Grandma knew I'd keep it this way. That's all. I'm doing this for her, for her memory."

Gwyneth drew herself up to her full height of five foot two, the same as Lily. The resemblance between them was considerable. Both had unmanageable, untamable, wavy light brown hair, matching light brown eyes and full mouths that looked great in lipstick.

But only Lily had a ready smile.

Gwyneth's mouth was turned down in a frown, as usual. "I wouldn't have gone against her wishes."

"I think you wouldn't *mean* to, but you'd have found a way to justify it. The ski hill's already at capacity on most weekends and our day lodge can't handle any more than that. You would need to build another lodge, and then you would want more rooms... It would never end. We'd become one of those big, impersonal places I hate."

"I'm not a bad person, Lily Rose."

Lily had to grin at that. "Bad is relative."

"As you would know."

"Absolutely. And by the way, there's nothing wrong with being bad once in a while."

Her sister sighed the sigh of a martyr. "I can't reason with you, you don't have normal reasoning. And all I've ever said about Bay Moon is that with a little expansion—"

"We'd make a killing," Lily finished for her. "That would be great, but it'd turn into something that Bay Moon was never intended to be." She was adamant on this. When she'd first been dumped here by her at-their-wits'-end parents, she'd had all rights rudely revoked. No phone, no TV, no car, no friends and especially no boys. She'd been forced to serve the guests and worked the shop, the cafeteria and the lifts, only getting to ski or board as often as she could sneak out.

As a result, no one knew better than she that the best part of Bay Moon was its size and charm. Like the fictional *Cheers* bar, everyone here knew everyone's name, their likes and dislikes. Expanding would turn it into another Park City or Vail, where no one knew anyone and it was all about fashion and who the celebrity guests were. That simply was *not* going to happen. "Grandma knew what you and Sara wanted to do with this place. Just as she knew that as the older, responsible granddaughters, you two were the logical choices to inherit. But the fact is, she left it all to me." A burden she'd neither coveted nor asked for. Hell, she'd have been happy working ski patrol the rest of her life.

"Yes, she left it all to you," Gwyneth said. "Even though you'd never held a business or finance position, didn't balance your own checkbook and had never had so much as a single lasting relationship in your life."

"And what do relationships have to do with anything?"

"Shows a lack of ability to commit, Lily."

No, it showed a lack of willingness to commit—a direct result of her bossy, demanding family. Love was a burden, Lily had long ago decided, and an unwelcome one. "Okay, listen. Let's save my failings for another time. Maybe Thanksgiving, when everyone can join in on the fun. For now, we have jobs, good ones. We make extremely good livings just the way things are."

"Yes." Gwyneth dropped her gaze over Lily's ski-patrol attire. "And I see you're going to be earning yours screwing off all day."

She'd already put in two hours at her desk, but hell if she'd defend herself. It didn't seem to matter what she said to Gwyneth, or how often she said it—her sister just refused to see the hours Lily was spending chained to her desk, the paperwork she was shoveling her way through or the results. Fine. She was done arguing. "Ski patrol is hardly screwing off."

"We have people for that."

"Never enough. Safety first," she said, imitating her grandma's mantra with a smile, refusing to be baited into admitting that while she loved this resort, the day-to-day running of it had been infringing on her enjoyment of the mountain for some time. Actually, it was sucking the soul right out of her.

"If you'd only listen to reason," Gwyneth said coolly.

"I don't have normal reasoning, remember?"

With a frustrated growl, Gwyneth whirled on her heels. "I'll be in my office."

No doubt terrorizing Carrie, their shared assistant, as she micromanaged the lot of them.

God, Lily missed her grandma with a physical ache. She missed the simple understanding. Her grandfather had been gone much longer and she missed him, too. Her parents weren't gone, just not around. Chin up, she pushed open the doors, sucked in the brisk twenty-degree air and stepped down the three wide stone steps to take in the glory around her.

Towering forests of pines heavy with snow, and steep, rocky valleys watched over by the awesome Sierras…it was an amazing celebration of contrasts, she thought, her breath crystallizing in front of her face. With a smile, she dropped her board to the snow and buckled a foot into her binding. The air was cold enough to burn her lungs as she inhaled.

She wasn't on the schedule to patrol today, just on call. She'd only put on her ski-patrol jacket to get past any siblings, and—with the exception of that little run-in with Gwyneth just now—her plan had worked. She was free.

And free was just what the doctor ordered.

She pushed off and headed down a small incline directly toward Sierra Gulch, the quad lift that would take her to midmountain. From there, she'd get on Upper Way, yet another lift, to the top of the mountain this time. And from there, she'd take whichever run caught her fancy.

She checked in on her walkie-talkie to patrol base. Danny, a patroller, told her to have fun. Not a problem.

It was barely eight-fifteen, and the chairs officially didn't run until eight-thirty, so there wasn't much of a line yet. With her jacket, and the white cross on the back denoting her as ski patrol, she was entitled to move ahead of everyone else, but she didn't. Unless there was an emergency, she didn't mind waiting in the lines, visiting with the people on what she considered "her" mountain.

She moved in behind a couple and their two young children. Another skier came up on her right. Craning her head intending to say hello, she felt a sudden jolt right down to her toes.

The man who'd caused the jolt smiled at her. And *whoa, baby*, but the way he did caused a rush of blood through her veins more thrilling than any first run on the slopes could give her.

Before she could return the smile, she was jostled from behind, and might have fallen flat on her face but for the man with the brain-cell-melting smile on her right. His gloved hand settled on her arm, holding her steady. Grinning her thanks, she used the moment to take a good look at him, at the dark, wavy hair that called to a woman's fingers, at the complexion that suggested both a tan and an Italian heritage and at the wide, firm mouth that immediately brought to mind a long night of hot sin.

She couldn't see the eyes behind his mirrored Oakleys, darn it, but at her lengthy perusal, he arched a slow brow. His smile became just a little heated, and in his easy stance she detected an edge, an aura of danger, a delicious, spine-tingling shiver of attitude.

God, she loved a fellow rebel.

And then there was his physique—all hard length and sleek power. His lightweight black jacket fit snugly to his broad shoulders and chest, loosely at the waist. His cargo ski pants were loose, too, but in no way hid the effect of his long legs. Here was a man who kept his body in prime condition—possibly an athlete.

Yum.

"Single?" he asked as the line shifted closer to the lift.

She knew he was asking if she was single for the lift, but she answered for both that *and* her personal life. "Very."

He smiled again, and together they moved to the front of the lift. The operator was Eric, a twenty-five-year-old ski bum who'd been running lifts for seven years now. He gave her the thumbs-up sign. "Drop Off, dudette."

"That's where I'm heading now." She couldn't wait to have the icy wind in her face, the feel of the slope beneath her.

"Drop Off?" the magnificent male specimen next to her asked as they sat on their chair, swinging into the air over a popular intermediate run called Calamity Alley.

The snow looked like endless yards of corduroy, thanks to the grooming crew working nights on the snowcats. "Drop Off is a run on the back side, off the north cornice," she said.

"Sounds like a good place to start."

"Oh, no," she said with a laugh. "It's a horrible place to start. It's a double-diamond run, expert only."

And the Sierras had been dumped on last night, making it all the more challenging. A blanket of fresh white powder lay as far as the eye could see, coating the trees on either side of the runs below like stoically swaying hundred-foot-high ghosts. Lily's adrenaline began to pump. She lived for powder days. Lived to huck herself off Drop Off, a two-and-a-half-mile run with a wicked three-thousand-foot vertical drop.

The man next to her pushed up his sunglasses, showing his eyes for the first time. *Melting chocolate,* was her first thought, and good Lord, but she was suddenly starving for some. "Double diamond?" he repeated.

"Yes. Have you been here before?"

He shifted his broad shoulders forward to adjust his narrow backpack to be more comfortable between his spine and the chair. "No."

"But you have skied before," she guessed, as evidenced by his ease getting on the lift.

"I do all right."

He certainly looked all right. More than. And yet, just because he did, didn't mean he was a good skier. She'd actually discovered that the more good-looking someone was, the less skill they required to get through life, skiing included.

Far too many times she'd been pulled in by a pretty face only to discover that all the expensive gear was merely a front. An illusion. Not that it had stopped her from enjoying said pretty face, but she understood and appreciated the fine art of one-night standing and happened to be extremely selective. It'd been a while since she'd indulged, but suddenly, looking into eyes the color of expensive, dark, rich mocha, she decided she was due.

Past due.

But whether she slept with him or not, she wouldn't have any casualties on her conscience. If this hunk of amazing flesh couldn't ski, she'd happily point him in the direction of the bunny slopes and go on her merry powder way. "I'll get you a map at the top so you can find the right runs for you."

"Thank you," he said, sounding amused. "But I can figure it out."

A bunch of loud catcalls and *woo-hoos* burst in the air. The four guys on the lift behind them had gotten a nice look at Calamity Alley, smooth and freshly groomed. They were young and exuberant, brimming with an unmitigated joy that was contagious enough to make Lily smile.

The devastating hottie next to her had shifted to look, too, putting an arm up along the back of the chair to do so. The material of his gear crinkled, and through the icy morning came the scent of his soap, his shampoo…and more. *Clean, pure male,* she thought with an inhale that had her nostrils quivering.

His eyes met hers, first with humor—he'd caught her sniffing him!—and then with an answering crackle of awareness and attraction. She just knew that he was thinking stuff, all sorts of wicked, unspeakable, bad-boy stuff, and suddenly the morning chill dissipated. She didn't look away, she couldn't, and neither did he. The moment stretched out, sizzling in intensity.

Far beneath them, a lone skier took the mountain in a series of long S-turns. She shifted her attention downward, nearly quivering, though now she wasn't sure it was just the need to follow the fall line on her own freshly waxed board that had her senses on full alert.

"You get down there a lot, I take it, since you're a local." He nodded to her ski-patrol jacket.

"Born and bred."

"You've been boarding a long time, then."

And skiing, too. Her grandpa had put her on a board at the tender age of two. She'd been a holy terror ever since, as any living member of her family could attest to. "How about you? Where are you from?"

"Ohio."

"Long way from home." She loved hearing their guests' stories. Plus, she just loved his voice, low and just a little husky. "So what brings you here, besides the wonderful resort and the fact we have the best skiing on the planet?"

"My partner gave me a week out here. Said I needed a vacation."

"Wow. Nice partner."

Before she could ask more, or what he did for a living, they were at the top of the lift. They got off together and skied forward to Upper Way, which would deposit them at the top of the world—or what felt like it at 11,150 feet. They got on with two boarders, who managed to get between her and her beautiful stranger, and this time there was little talk and lots of awe as they all took in the stunning Sierras in full winter splendor.

When they finally reached the top, Lily stopped to wave to the lift operator and pulled her sunglasses out from inside her jacket.

The two boarders quickly vanished down the front of Surprise, a lovely, groomed intermediate run that would eventually take them back to the midmountain lift. Her mysterious rebel had shifted forward, meanwhile, to read the large billboard map that exhibited all the runs. A dry-erase board beneath it listed which of them had been groomed and their conditions. He bent to tighten his boots—which gave her the chance to notice that his butt was as extremely fine as the rest of him—then he straightened and pushed off, heading toward the back side and Drop Off.

"Hey," she called out, but it was too late. "Damn it." She went after him. At the lip of the run, she hastily bent and locked her other foot into her binding. He'd already begun his descent, and as she watched, her mouth fell open. He'd said he was an "all right" skier, but the man was beyond anything even close to all right. In fact, he moved like poetry in motion, perfectly in sync with the fall line of the mountain. Was that ever sexy.

With a grin of anticipation and lust and pure joy, she threw herself off the edge of her world, flying down the mountain after him.

2

LILY PASSED HER HOT MAN In Black, waving as she swooshed on by. The beauty of Drop Off was its combination of sheer length and vertical drop, never failing to give her a roller-coaster, stomach-to-her-toes feeling—but today the run had an extra edge to it, courtesy of her sizzling audience.

The trees on either side of the sharp, creviced run blurred as her eyes watered with the icy morning chill. Still she pushed harder, happily losing herself in speed and adrenaline.

Halfway down, she leaped into a quick stop and, as she often liked to do, turned to look back up at the cliff she'd just taken. Breath coming in quick, short pants, she swiped at her glasses to rid them of the flakes of powder blocking her view.

He skied up beside her, stopping close enough to spray her with snow. "Still worried about me?"

She shot him a droll look. "You failed to mention you were expert."

He let out a slow grin. "You failed to ask."

True.

"Race to the bottom?" he asked casually.

The bad girl in her screamed, *Oh, yes*! But the sensible ski patroller in her demurred. "Racing on a hill not denoted for such things isn't wise."

Hc laughed, a sound that scraped low in her belly. "And here I thought you were so tough."

She stared into his teasing eyes and nearly drowned in the dark orbs. "*Tough* and *stupid* aren't synonyms."

"We both know you're dying to race me." Leaning in close, he whispered, "I dare you."

He had no way of knowing that she loved a good dare, that she'd never turned one down in her life. Not in second grade, when Tony Villa had dared her to put superglue on their teacher's chair. Not in sixth grade, when Eric Orlando had dared her to pull down her pants and moon the baseball team. Even though a dare had led her right down the wrong path many, many more times than she could count she'd long ago given up fighting the lust for life that throbbed in her veins. She looked around to make sure they were alone. "I'll show you 'tough.'"

His grin was slow and wicked. "Are we on, then?"

"You bet your sweet ass." With no one in sight, making the dare okay in her books, she blew him a little kiss, then leaped forward, going balls out, straight down the mountain. She could hear him on her tail, and then he was right next to her, and for long moments they stayed like that, side by side, the swooshing of the snow beneath his skis and her board a wonderful sound.

Finally she edged free just a little and eyeballed the next sharp turn. *I can take him right here, I can pull ahead—*

Her walkie-talkie chirped, and with a grand sigh

for what might have been, she stopped short and answered the call. "Go ahead," she said to base.

"Skier disappeared out-of-bounds, on the north face between Surprise and Drop Off. Friends say he has no business being out-of-bounds, and he's not responding to shout-outs. Danny said you're already up there."

"I'm on Drop Off. I'll ski between the trees to get over there, see if I can see him."

"Chris is on his way, too."

Chris had her old, beloved position of Patrol Director, and loved the mountain as much as she did. He, too, was only on call today, but undoubtedly hadn't been able to resist the fresh snow any more than she had. She clipped the radio back onto her belt and eyed the trees off to her right, knowing she could board through the tightly growing pines and come out just above the area where the skier had gone out-of-bounds. Or so she hoped. She turned to go, then remembered. She wasn't alone. She eyed her perfect stranger's long, most excellent form.

"You think he's lost?"

"Or down," she said. "And hurt."

"And so off you go."

"Yeah. Sorry about the race. Maybe we can give it another shot later."

He nodded, and with a good amount of regret, Lily took off through the trees, which in itself was an adventure on a board with a foot of fresh powder. With the pines packed so close to each other and this part of the mountain so incredibly steep, even experienced skiers ran into serious trouble here.

But because she knew the entire hill like the back of her hand, she came out of the trees just above the out-of-bounds area on the north face, which consisted of a steep cliff overlooking a valley of rough, unskiable terrain. Despite that and the clear boundary markers, there were still a few yahoos every year who tried to ski out this way.

Traversing along the edge a little bit, she indeed found a set of tracks. Someone had skied down right here and gone off the edge. She stared at the sign that read Unpatrolled Beyond This Point, Out-Of-Bounds Territory and shook her head. "Idiot," she muttered. She used her walkie-talkie to check in with base and was clipping it back to her belt when she heard a skier coming. Puzzled, she turned to face Sexy Man In Black.

"I followed your track." He stood with ease on his skis, white powder dusting halfway up his long legs. "You going down here?"

"Yeah."

His smile was gone, replaced by an intensity that took her breath every bit as much as his good humor had. "Be safe."

"You, too. Careful getting out of here." She pushed off.

The terrain was even steeper than Drop Off had been, the way uneven, with the double threat of sheer rock and unmarked cliffs, not to mention the possibility of an avalanche. Granted, there'd been a patrolling team out at five this morning, checking on that very threat, but you couldn't be too careful.

Or too careless. This area was unpatrolled for a

good reason, and as she maneuvered her way along, following the tracks of the missing skier, she cursed him for putting even more people in jeopardy with his foolishness.

She pulled up short just before a heart-stopping cliff, gratified to see the tracks ahead veer off to the left. Again, she pulled out her walkie-talkie and verified with base that she was in the correct vicinity, had his tracks in sight and that, so far, he hadn't fallen down the cliff. At least not this one.

"I think I see him."

Jerking in surprise, she once again turned and met a dark, chocolate gaze. "What the hell are you doing following me?"

"Helping," he said simply.

He was an even better skier than she'd thought if he'd gotten here without a problem. "Look, this is crazy stuff. It's one thing for me to put myself on the line to find a thoughtless idiot, but you don't need to or have to. Now, seriously, stop. Stay. I don't want to have to worry about you, too."

"I'm SAR," he said, and when she just stared at him, he clarified, "Search and Rescue."

"I know what SAR means." Hmm. She didn't have time to analyze the little skip in her pulse, nor did she know what to make of him, a man clearly as insane as she was.

"I can help," he said.

Lily was very used to the people in her world trying to rein her in, hold her back, telling her she couldn't, she shouldn't, constantly reminding her how much of a screwup she'd been all her life—

which, perversely, always made her want to step over the proverbial line. Or erase it.

But now, for the first time ever, *she* had the urge to rein someone in, to tell them *they* couldn't, they shouldn't, and she had to admit that it was majorly unnerving. She wanted to grab him, make him wait, make sure that he didn't get hurt, that he stayed safe. Was that how her family felt? "Okay, so you're trained, but this is my rescue—"

"There." He pointed, then pushed past her to actually beat her to the rescue. Only about twenty-five yards straight down the vertical slope, a skier sat on a rock, looking a little sheepish as he lifted one foot, minus the ski he'd clearly lost into the vast valley below.

With one last sigh, Lily followed.

THE RESCUE WENT WELL, THE lecture given, the reports filled out, and before Lily knew it, the whole incident was over.

And her mystery man was gone.

She'd never even learned his name. Her pride chafed a little at that, and the fact that apparently he hadn't felt the need to learn hers, even though he'd been the one to use the small first-aid kit in her fanny pack to treat a wound on the lost skier's knee. He'd chatted with the young punk, joking about how he'd been given this trip while at a bachelor party for his best friend and about how much easier skiing was than rappelling out of helicopters, or flying them, which he apparently did on a daily basis in his SAR duties.

Watching him work had been an interesting experience. He had such an easygoing confidence and an authority that didn't grate or grind on her nerves. That had been a first.

Still, she knew she hadn't imagined the scorching heat in his eyes every time he'd looked at her, so if he was stupid enough to let her go, well, then, he could just damn well suffer for it.

Back in her office, she worked for several hours solid on her least favorite chore—paperwork. Even a small resort like Bay Moon generated mountains of it, all of which had to be done, though she'd have preferred to be outside on the real mountain. Trying not to resent it, she approved the budget for the ski shop's fall stock, looked over Sara's guest-services report and eyed the accounting reports for Gwyneth. *Ugh.*

Finally, she glanced at the clock. Three o'clock. A good time for the lunch she'd never had, she figured, and popped out of her office.

"You going out for a bite?" Carrie asked. She was a local, like Lily, who'd spent years enjoying her ultimate-ski-bunny status, until two years ago when she'd fallen on the slopes and tweaked her lower back. Now she occasionally skied a beginner slope, but mostly worked in the office, enjoying her great view, with an unbelievably good attitude.

If Lily had lost her ability to board or ski, she wouldn't have been nearly so accepting. "Yeah, I'm going out."

Carrie grinned. "Let me guess—you're going to the midlodge for a burger."

She was going to the midlodge, all right, but she wouldn't be stopping for a burger. She'd be getting on yet another lift to get to the top of the hill for a few runs before they closed. "Mmm...maybe."

"It's snowing again."

"Since when has that ever been a deterrent?" But she did dodge back into her office to trade her sunglasses for her goggles, grabbing them off their perch on her desk lamp.

Carrie's laugh rang out as Lily left. "Ski one for me, would you?"

"You got it." The lodge was full of skiers and boarders, all talking, some eating, and by the looks of it, everyone enjoying themselves. Lily found herself smiling as she walked through and went outside. Small flakes drifted lazily down as she got on the lift.

She'd no sooner gotten off at midmountain when she came across a fight between two boarders who turned out to be identical-twin fools. They were fighting over which run to take, and had gathered an audience. Lily swore, tossed aside her board and leaped in, pushing them apart, but not before she took an elbow to her chin, making her see stars. "You," she growled, jabbing one in the chest. They were about twenty years old, lanky and looking a little worse for the fight in the snow. "You okay?"

He touched a growing bruise under his eye and glared at his twin. "Yeah."

"That's too bad," she said, then whirled when his brother snickered. "Listen carefully. Go down Calamity Alley, go around the lodge, *not* through, and straight to your car."

"Calamity Alley," he whined. "That's nothing but a bunny hill."

She swiped her finger over his season pass hanging around his neck. "Go, or lose this."

"Hey, I paid good money for that!" He pulled free. "You can't tell me what to do."

Her chin throbbed, and every moment that passed meant less time on the slopes before she had to go back inside. "See this jacket? It means I can tell you whatever I want." She gestured down the hill. "Don't come back today." She turned to his brother. "And you. Go down Abby's Lane, which runs parallel to Calamity Alley. Same rules. Around the lodge, *not* through, and don't come back today or you'll lose *your* season pass."

A long, tense moment passed while they shot her matching sullen looks. With a few of their buddies egging them on behind her, she turned in a circle in the lightly falling snow, hand on her walkie-talkie, wondering if she'd have to call for backup, which would just really top it for her.

Then a man pushed his way through the small crowd to stand beside her, and her heart hit her throat.

Her Sexy Man In Black.

He'd replaced his sunglasses with goggles, as well, but other than that, looked the same. Which was to say, knee-knockingly good. He took in the situation with one quick, sweeping gaze, then settled that gaze on her, silently offering support while letting her remain in charge.

She eyed the twins again, but after a minute they both huffed out a breath. "It's snowing anyway," one muttered, and they went their separate ways with matching grumbles. Only then did she let herself relax as her gaze once again collided with a dark, melting-chocolate one.

"Fun stuff," he said.

"Yeah. Sometimes it's Idiot Central around here."

He flashed a devastating grin that revved her engines. "You handled it."

Yeah, she had, but that he'd noticed and given her credit for it made her take a good long second look at him. And a third. "You having a good day?"

"Oh, yeah. And seeing you again is a nice bonus, too."

She bent to tighten the laces on her boots, giving herself a moment because the man seriously scrambled her brain, even more so now that she knew he wasn't just an arresting face and hot bod. He had brains to go with both. And that he worked in SAR just upped the gotta-have-him factor because there was nothing, absolutely nothing, hotter than a guy capable of putting his life on the line to rescue another.

She both felt and heard him ski closer, his edges scraping into the groomed snow at his short stop. When she straightened, he was right there, facing the opposite direction to her, skis parallel to her board. Close enough to touch.

He took off his right glove. Reaching out, his jacket crinkling as it shifted over his broad shoulders, he touched her bruised chin.

"I'm okay," she said.

He simply pulled her shaded goggles off her face.

"What?" she asked, squinting through the falling snow.

"I wanted to see your eyes."

Hmm. Figuring turnabout was fair play, she tugged his goggles off, as well.

The air crackled as they looked at each other. Then he rocked back on his heels and let out a breath. "I thought maybe I'd imagined it."

"Imagined...?"

Her jacket was unzipped to her breastbone, with only a thermal silk scoop-neck undershirt beneath. With a light touch, he put his bare finger to the pulse racing at the base of her throat. "This."

3

ALL LILY COULD HEAR WAS the thump, thump, thumping of her heart beating too fast in her ears. Her clothes felt too tight—or maybe that was her own skin. A heavy anticipation filled the cold air and she tried to tell herself it was something she'd felt often. Had acted on often.

But today, with this man, it felt startlingly, shockingly different.

Again he ran the pad of his finger over her pulse.

She took some comfort in the fact his own, beating at his throat, was no more steady than hers. "This...what?" she asked.

Something flashed in his eyes. Impatience? "I'm not sure I can put it into words without getting too graphic."

Her body let out a shiver, and honest to God, her knees wobbled. "I see." At least her voice was steady. "Does this happen to you often?"

"No. You?"

Feeling as if she could dive into his eyes and happily drown? Wanting to rip her clothes off and take his hands and put them on her body, sure she would die if he didn't hurry? "No," she managed. "Not often."

His gaze danced over her, from her boots to her legs, her body, her helmet, beneath which her hair was contained in a scrunchie at her shoulder blades. Finally, he met her eyes.

She knew she was nothing that special or extraordinary, and yet when he just kept looking his fill, she found herself squirming. *"What?"*

Now he stroked that finger carefully over her jaw. "At the rescue this morning, I heard the other patrollers refer to you as Slim, but that's not your name."

"No. It's Lily Harmon."

"Logan White." His hand moved from her jaw around to the nape of her neck, where he tugged lightly, playfully, on her ponytail. "You've had a long day already, Lily Harmon."

"And yet, given all I have left to do, it's only just begun."

"An overachiever?"

She laughed. Wouldn't her sisters get a kick out of that accusation? "Not quite." His shoulders blocked her view of anything but him, something she found she didn't mind in the least.

"Are you still on duty?" he asked.

"I never really was when it comes to ski patrol today, I'm only on call. I…uh, work in the lodge." *I own it*. A fact she usually kept to herself because it changed people's perceptions, which in turn pissed her off. "I'm on a late lunch break."

"That works."

Anticipation quivered through her veins as the snow continued to fall lightly. She thought of all the things they could do on the rest of her break, none of which involved eating. At least not food. "Works for what exactly?"

"Well, we never finished our little run on Drop Off. You still think you can beat me?"

She stared at him, then had to laugh. A race on the hill. Not ripping off their clothes. Right. "Oh, I know I can beat you."

His eyes flashed with the challenge and that in turn set off a little chain reaction of excitement within her. "Let's go," she said.

They took the lift, then made their way to the top of the run and looked down at the sharp incline. There were only a few skiers scattered on it, and they were moving quickly out of sight.

"Ready?" he asked.

"Oh, yeah." She buckled herself into her binding. "Prepare to lose."

He laughed, a low, sexy sound she could grow extremely attached to. "We'll see about that—"

She didn't wait for him to finish his sentence before she pushed off. Cheating? Only slightly. Besides, she'd seen him ski now, and truthfully, she wasn't all that positive she actually could beat him, unless she caught him by surprise in some way.

As the wind whistled past her, the thrill of the run settled in and her heart started pumping in a staccato beat. He caught up, and for a while they were neck and neck in the falling snow, the only sound being the *swoosh, swoosh* of their equipment pushing at the powder snow.

Evenly matched, she thought with a rush. They were shockingly evenly matched.

Would they be so evenly matched in bed?

Just as the errant thought entered her head, a lone skier suddenly vaulted into action ahead of them, not looking, moving too quickly and recklessly on the trail as it narrowed to a width that allowed for only one person safely at a time. Lily edged ahead of Logan and slowed them both down as she realized the other skier was completely, totally, out of control going into the turn. Even as she thought it, he skidded and began to slide toward the sharp drop-off. "Hey!" she called. "Slow down!"

The skier jerked at her voice and, clearly realizing he wasn't going to make the turn, went down in a tumble on his skis rather than fall over the cliff.

Lily began to board around him, planning on getting below him to stop and check that he was okay. But he struggled to get up, all scrambled arms and legs, managing to hook her with his pole as she went into her stop, tripping her into a dive.

She felt herself heading, airborne, directly toward the edge and the falling that waited past it, but then she was landing hard, in a tangle of limbs that weren't her own.

Logan. He sat up, quickly reaching for her. "You okay?"

No, she was not. She'd fallen. *Fallen.* She never fell, damn it. She spit out a mouthful of snow and looked around, realizing he'd taken her down purposely, catching her inches from the cliff. Her stomach wobbled at the damage the rocks might have done to her body if he hadn't been so quick-thinking on his skis. Before she could stand, he wrapped his fingers around her arm and held her still. "That was a helluva dive. Make sure you're okay first."

The only thing hurting was her pride, and she pulled free. "I'm fine." She looked over her shoulder in time to catch the out-of-control skier bolt down the mountain, without so much as a backward look.

"Nice," Logan said drily.

"Most are." She stood and looked down at her left boot, no longer buckled onto her board. Great. "I broke the binding." Snapped it right off, actually, which was nothing her screwdriver could fix. The prospect of having to walk down the damn mountain only added insult to injury.

"Hang on." Logan shrugged out of his backpack and opened it, burrowing through the contents.

"A roll of duct tape?" she asked incredulously when he held it up.

"Watch." Then he proceeded to pull a total *Mac-Gyver*, using the tape to rig the board's binding to hold her boot. "No more hotshot stuff," he warned, stepping back so that she could buckle herself in. "Don't want to push it."

She stood there brushing herself off, torn between annoyance and a telling pain in her left knee. It was an old injury, and surgery, twice, had repaired it, but damn if it didn't suddenly ache like a son of a bitch.

"Let's take a minute," he said, watching her closely.

Hating the weakness, she forced a smile. "Why, are you tired?"

"Lily—"

The walkie-talkie at her hip went off, and anything the two of them might have said or done was put on hold as Sara's voice filled the air. She was the middle sister, two years younger than Gwyneth. Instead of cold, cynical and bossy, she was mothering, nosy and bossy. "Lily Rose, I'm at your desk, and you're not here."

"Amazing powers of deduction," Lily muttered.

"Lily Rose? Can you hear me?"

She might be a badass to the rest of the world, but to Sara and Gwyneth, she was the eternal baby sister. "What's up?"

"You need a maid. My God, your desk is a disaster."

"Thanks. I'll be down in a few," she said into the walkie-talkie.

Less than five seconds later, her cell phone rang. She didn't have to look to see it was Sara. "What now?" she said when she'd hit speakerphone rather than take off her helmet so that she could hear.

"I just wanted to tell you something." Sara spoke with slow care, a sure sign she was miffed. "Two things. Aunt Debbie showed up earlier. She skied a while and now wants a suite."

"Well, you're guest services. Check with your reservations desk, but I'm sure both our suites are taken this week."

"They are. She's making a stink, saying she told you to clear one for her."

Aunt Debbie was their mother's younger sister, their grandma's "surprise," a late-in-life baby, and was only a few years older than Gwyneth. A born diva, she lived in New York, but always came out to ski once a year or so, wearing the finest designer gear, bearing embarrassingly expensive gifts and smothering hugs. She'd spend the time hanging around the lodge looking rich and beautiful, always choosing some particular spectacular ski stud to hook up with for the week.

Certainly if Aunt Debbie had told Lily she'd planned on coming to ski this week, Lily would have remembered to take an Advil in advance. "Well, she didn't. Just give her the best room you can come up with."

"I will, but, sweetie, you really need to remember these things or ask for help if you need it."

Lily banged the phone on her forehead. Talking to her sisters was like talking to two particularly impenetrable brick walls.

"Oh, and Gwyneth says an old friend is coming in tonight for a week's stay with his brand-new Jeep." There was laughter in Sara's voice now. "And that you're not to steal it, as is your habit with Jeeps."

Instead of banging her head again, Lily tipped her head back and looked at the sky, into the snow falling out of it like angel drops. It'd been ten years since she'd been arrested for stealing a Jeep. "Didn't you get the bulletin? I don't steal *new* Jeeps. Only old ones."

Sara chortled. "Sorry. I couldn't resist."

Lily disconnected. "Aren't you funny."

"Older sister?"

Lily tentatively flexed and bounced on her knee, testing. Not good. "Yeah. She hasn't grasped the fact that I'm no longer a wild child and that stealing Dad's precious Jeep Laredo to go smoke weed on Mole Hill just doesn't hold the same appeal."

Logan laughed and once again pulled off his backpack, unzipping it. "Ah, the fond memories of our stupid youths."

Impressed that he didn't ask her a million questions about her past, she watched him kneel in the snow and shift through his pack. "Granted," she admitted. "I had more stupid moments than most."

"Because you got caught?" He pulled out an elastic bandage.

"It wasn't difficult that time. I forgot to set the emergency brake, and when I got out to sit on the cliffs to smoke and watch the moon, the truck rolled down the mountain."

"Ouch."

"Yeah." She sighed. "And now I'm that stupid kid forever, no matter how many years I put between me and my...indiscretions."

"I take it you're the baby of the family?"

"Unfortunately." She eyed him as he came close once again, tossing the bandage up and down in his hand. "And you?"

"The oldest."

"Ah." She smiled. "So are you an impossible, cold, hard know-it-all?"

"Undoubtedly."

Slowly she shook her head. "You might be impossible, and the know-it-all part remains to be seen, but I don't buy the cold."

He ignored that and nodded to her leg. "What's with the knee?"

"See? Cold wouldn't have even noticed." She came clean when he didn't give up an ounce of the intensity. "Ancient injury."

Crouching before her in the snow, he pulled her Gore-Tex pants up to her thigh while she silently thanked herself for shaving that morning. Then he bent his dark head. His breath danced over her skin. With his index finger, he traced the six-inch scar that rounded her kneecap in a half circle. His finger was warm and callused.

"It's old," she said.

"Not that old. Want the wrap?"

What she wanted wrapped was his body around hers, but she wasn't too stubborn to admit the bandage would give her the support she needed to get down the hill. "Please."

Tipping his face up, he smiled at her in a way that suggested he knew accepting help from anyone went against the grain. Still holding her gaze, he tugged his gloves off with his teeth, an oddly erotic thing all in itself. Then he peeled her ski sock down.

She hissed.

He went still. "Hurt?"

"Your hands are cold."

He flashed a grin. "Suck it up." With efficiency, he wrapped her knee, then pulled her sock back up and her pant leg down over her boot. "You should soak it when we get back. Do employees get to use the hot tub?"

"Actually..." She stared down at him, into those amazing eyes. It was unusual, and it made no sense, but she wanted him to know the truth. She wanted him to know her. "I'm not quite an employee."

He straightened, standing a good head taller than her. "No?"

"No. I, um…" She smiled wryly. "I own the resort. Inherited it, actually."

He didn't even blink. "So I'm taking it you get access to the hot tub."

She stared at him, then laughed. Still no ridiculously invasive questions, not a single joke, none of the usual stuff that always so completely and totally irritated her when she revealed that she, a twenty-five-year-old punk, owned a ski resort.

"Can you board down with your knee?" he asked.

As her other option was lying in a litter while a pair of her patrollers took her down the mountain, she nodded. Though she went slower this time, he didn't try to pass her or continue their race. Instead, he followed, presumably to help her if she needed it. And though she'd skied with plenty of men she'd planned on sleeping with over the years, she'd never felt so…aware of one as she was of Logan.

The slopes were filled with skiers heading down to the lodge on their last run of the day as the sun began to sink. Halfway back, her walkie-talkie chirped again. It was Chris this time, with a new emergency on the east side. A boarder had fallen out-of-bounds. He was uninjured but unable to climb back up the sheer rock to safety.

"Just shoot me now," Lily muttered, then lifted an apologetic gaze to Logan. "Fun's over. *Again*. I have patrollers on their way, but I'm going over to help."

"Whoever you were talking to sounded worried."

"It's going to be a little tricky getting him back up. It's getting dark. And where he went over is sheer rock, covered in two months' worth of ice, topped with some powder."

"Avalanche waiting to happen."

"You got it," she said grimly. "There are signs making it out-of-bounds for exactly that reason."

"Maybe I can help."

"No."

"I have ten years' climbing experience."

She let out a breath. He'd fixed her binding. With duct tape. He'd wrapped her knee when most wouldn't have even known she'd been hurt. Mr. Safety and Security, she'd give him that, and yet he willingly threw himself into any risk.

Damn if that wasn't unbearably sexy all by itself. "All right, fine. You're hired. Let's go, ace."

"Okay, Lily Rose."

She arched a brow. "Use my middle name again and you'll be the one left out-of-bounds."

His laughter rang out in the snow-filled air and made her smile.

4

LOGAN WATCHED LILY'S PETITE form glide down the steep incline in the snow, doing so far more purposefully and carefully than she had earlier. He wondered just how badly she'd hurt herself.

He could hear Wyatt now... *You can take the man out of the SAR team but you can't take the SAR team out of the man.*

Yeah, yeah, sue him. After a lifetime of watching after his two younger siblings for his overworked father, and then working search and rescue, taking care of others was nothing but pure instinct for him.

Granted, she was tough as hell and damned upfront and practical to boot, and could undoubtedly take care of herself—but that didn't stop him from wanting to make sure.

And then there was the searing heat that shot back and forth between them like a Ping-Pong ball with every glance, every word. She might not be the drop-dead beautiful ski bunny Wyatt had had in mind for him, but she had a secret sort of try-me smile and a way about her that was far more sensual than any woman he'd been with in a long time.

They got to the lift they needed to take and headed

back up again. In less than ten minutes they were standing at the lip of another dizzy drop-off where their skier had fallen, with four other patrollers who were dealing with the victim's freaked-out friends, all of whom were eventually convinced to go wait at the lodge. The patrollers had already determined that their victim, down the precipice about forty feet, wasn't hurt. Now they were trying to figure out where the out-of-bounds signs had gone.

"Just this morning, three of them were spread right here across the cliff," Lily said, baffled.

"They're gone now." One of the patrollers scratched his head. "Hard to blame the guy for getting into trouble when he didn't know he was heading into it."

"Oh, no. No excuses. Anyone in his right mind would know to stay off this cliff." Lily shook her head. "But still, this looks bad."

"Some stupid punk prank," Chris said, setting up a strobe light to help them see in the growing dark. "Someone thought they were funny."

"What do you think?" Lily asked. "Take him down from there, or back up on a rope?"

"Either way," Chris said, "it's going to be a tricky rescue."

They knew what they were doing, Logan told himself as he stood there silently, but he itched to pitch in and help.

Another call came over the radio. Seemed the identical-twin troublemakers hadn't followed Lily's directions and were now fighting on the front lodge steps. Adding to the problem was the crowd of their buddies hooting and hollering and urging them on, and an increasingly aggressive crowd.

Looking royally pissed, Lily nodded for three of the crew to go down and handle it, leaving just her and Chris. The snow kept coming down, plus it wouldn't be long before they'd need the lights—daylight was fading fast, already impeding vision. "I'll go after this idiot," she said, resigned.

"Skiing out from there will be tough going," Chris said. "And we'd have to send a snowcat to pick you up, which'll pull someone away from another post. We're already short-staffed."

"It'll be a climb back up, then." She began to gear up with the harness and ropes the others had left. "Can you set up some caution tape to close off this area until we find the signs?"

Watching her, Logan discovered he couldn't sit back any longer. "Let me go down for him," he said.

"Logan—"

"Your knee might give out on you on the way back up. I've done this a thousand times. More."

"In the snow? On ice?"

"In the snow, on ice," he assured her. Maybe not at this altitude, and not at a ski resort, but so what? He could do this, more safely than she could at the moment.

She looked at her patroller. "Chris, you should officially meet Logan. He's SAR out of Ohio, a helicopter and rappelling expert. We can use his help, yes?"

"Are you kidding? *Yes.*"

"Hey!" came a faint cry from over the cliff. "You guys ever coming for me or what?"

Lily rolled her eyes at Chris, then leaned over the edge in a way that suggested a great ease with heights and an even greater confidence in herself. "Are you injured?"

"No! Just cold!"

"I'm coming." She grabbed the ropes but her walkie-talkie chirped again, and at the news from Danny at base she swore softly. They had a kid on his last run of the day with a broken wrist on the bunny slope, leaving her team stretched thin and thinner. "Chris—"

"I can't leave you alone, Slim."

"I've got Logan."

Logan moved in. "I'll do whatever's necessary."

Chris agreed reluctantly and turned to Lily. "Rappel down to him, but risk the ski-out, since you don't have enough manpower to pull you back up. Keep on the radio. I'll send in a snowcat to pick you up at the bottom."

"And then there were two," Lily said to Logan when Chris had left.

"My knee's good enough for what needs to be done." She prepared to rappel over the edge. "Don't let me fall."

He looked at her in horror. "I won't."

She smiled. "That was a joke, Logan. Gotta lighten up some. After I'm safely down, send my board down, too, then maybe you could gather the ropes for me and shut off the light. I'll ski the guy down to meet the cat."

And with that, she was gone. Totally trusting, believing in him, confident in her own abilities to make this thing happen.

She had to be the most amazing woman he'd ever met in his entire life. But that thought would have to wait because he now had her hanging off a sheer, icy cliff in questionable weather, her life in his very hands.

How many times had *he* put his own life in his teammates' hands and never given it another thought? Hundreds. *Thousands.* So he had no idea why his stomach had fallen to somewhere near his toes, with his heart in his throat, where it firmly remained until she signaled to him that she had reached the victim.

He sent down her board, then pulled up the ropes, gathering them so that he could ski with them looped over his shoulder. When he took another look over the edge, Lily and her rescue vic were already gone. Safe, he hoped, knowing they were moving down harsh, unwelcoming terrain not meant for humans.

Logan quickly taped off the area and shut down the light. He waited for his eyes to adjust to the growing twilight, and then began his own descent, on the regulated, patrolled slope closest to the rescue, stopping only half a minute later when an odd flicker of reflection came from the cluster of trees to his right. Skiing off the trail, about five feet in, between two tight trees, he found three signs.

Three "out of bounds" signs. He gathered them up, tucked them under his arm and, with the ropes still looped over his shoulder, headed down again, not stopping until he was at the lodge, standing in front of the first-aid cabin to its right, listening to the radio conversation between a patroller on a snowcat and Lily.

He was relieved when he heard she'd been picked

up, but had to wait another fifteen minutes before she came into view, looking tired and in some pain.

"Hey," she said in surprise at the sight of him hanging out on the covered deck. She lit up with pleasure, which froze on her face when she saw the signs lying at his feet.

"The area's taped off—and I found these just off the trail," he said.

"So some punk really moved them on purpose. Damn. Hard to remember if I was ever that stupid. Thanks for putting the tape up—and bringing these down." She picked up her walkie-talkie and asked someone to come get the signs and put them back where they belonged in the morning, before the hill opened to the public.

"You okay?" Logan asked when she was done.

"Sure. You didn't have to wait for me. I don't want you to waste your ski time on me."

Hadn't anyone ever waited for her? Made her feel like she was worth waiting for? "I just wanted to make sure your knee was okay—"

"I'm a big girl."

Yeah, he was getting that. Getting that she had to be. She was also intelligent, quick-witted and strong as hell.

She stepped off the covered deck into the lightly falling snow, then turned toward him, opening her mouth to catch a snowflake on her tongue.

A tongue he suddenly, desperately, wanted in his mouth. "You're sure you're not hurt?" He moved off the deck to stand next to her. They were alone, and because of it, he stepped even closer.

"What are you going to do if I am?" she asked in a daring voice as she caught yet another snowflake on her tongue. "Kiss it better?"

"Maybe."

"I dare you."

Without hesitation, he hauled her up against him to do just that and covered her mouth with his.

Her surprised murmur filled his head, along with the ensuing heat when the kiss went instantly hot and sweet all at once, sending hunger and desire skittering through his veins. He rocked against her, and with another surprised murmur, she opened her mouth to his, clutching him close.

Close was good, even if they were separated by clothing and gear. The material was designed to insulate, but none of it was a match for the heat that zapped between them. The pressure of her body, the glide of her tongue with his, gave him a glimpse of both heaven and hell. Heaven because he couldn't remember a better kiss than this, hell because he wasn't going to get much more, not out here in the open as they were.

But God, she fit against him so absolutely, as if she'd been made for him, and he fisted his hand on her jacket, low at her spine, rather than explore her curves and heat in public. After one more slow exploration of her delicious mouth, he forced himself to pull back, letting out a groan when her lips clung to his before letting go with a little suction sound that made him even harder.

Mouth still wet, she stared up at him, her eyes soft and aroused and touchingly unsure, as if she, too,

knew that this was different—and far more terrifying because of it. Then the expression was gone and
her cocky grin flashed. "Thanks for the help today,
ace. It's always nice to work with another adrenaline
junkie. You ever want to change locations, you're
hired."

His heart was still threatening to burst out of his
chest but he managed to answer. "I'm not an adrenaline junkie."

That made her laugh. "Anyone who willingly
throws himself into a situation like you have—
twice—is an adrenaline junkie." She smoothed her
fingers over his jaw with a smile. "Don't look so un-
settled. You should know, we can't help ourselves."
Leaning in, she bit his lower lip. "I gotta go."

The snow felt cold on his hot skin. "Your knee—"

"Feels better already. Have fun tonight."

And then she was gone.

LOGAN SKIED HARD THE NEXT day, wanting to clear his
mind. The day before had been interesting, educa-
tional and, to say the least, intriguing, and he had a
whole new appreciation for what someone like Lily
did for a living.

He also had a whole new appreciation for the
woman herself. Curvy, small as hell and with guts to
boot—he couldn't get her out of his mind. The wild
kiss hadn't helped. She'd thrown herself into that,
too, as she apparently threw herself into everything.

Did she have any idea how incredibly arousing
that was? Since he hadn't seen her once since, he had
no idea but he suspected she'd felt it, as well, and had

backed away from both that and him. He didn't miss the irony of that—a woman unnerved by nothing being unnerved by his kiss.

By the time late afternoon settled in, it looked more like twilight, with the sun behind the clouds. Snow drifted down, reflecting off the already white mountain. Around him the landscape took on a surreal feeling, almost as if he was standing on a movie set where everything had been painted white, with low lights added to make it all glow. It was also incredibly quiet, eerily so, because the snow hit with no sound at all, muffling all the other normal noises.

In that oddly beautiful winter wonderland, Logan skied to the lodge steps and removed his skis. For the second night in a row, he had absolutely nothing ahead of him to do, no one waiting on him, no paperwork, nothing. He could hardly wrap his mind around that.

He took the time to admire his surroundings. He loved the look of the lodge, a two-story sprawling cabin-style building wrapped in dark wood siding above a brick base, with at least one large outdoor patio off the east side. The myriad of windows were all trimmed in white with open shutters, giving the lodge a gingerbread-house kind of charm and personality. As he walked up the steps and under the hanging Bay Moon sign, stomping the snow off his boots, the doors opened and several skiers spilled out. So did the scent of all sorts of foods from the cafeteria, and his stomach growled, reminding him he'd skipped lunch. He stepped inside.

Off to the right and down a wide stone staircase

was a wing of guest rooms. Straight ahead lay the wide, open common room, and to the left, another hallway, where he could head into the cafeteria, the bar or the ski rental shop.

In the common room, a wide variety of people sat around the crackling flames contained in the huge stone fireplace. Several of the loungers were of the hot-ski-bunny variety that Wyatt had figured he'd be spending time enjoying.

The whole SAR team had spent the past few weeks razzing Logan about this trip, taking bets on how many women he could meet and if—when— any of them would stick.

He could have told them when.

Never.

In his world, love didn't stick at all, not when pitted against such a demanding lifestyle. His mother hadn't stuck with his father's nomadic military way of life, and had left her three young children early on. Many of his friends had been through women like cheap wine, and several were on second or third marriages. Any relationships Logan himself had attempted self-destructed when he'd proven he loved his job more than any significant other in his life.

He looked over the women in front of the fire, several of whom looked him over right back. A particularly tall, beautiful brunette smiled slowly at him, her eyes eating him up.

A ski bunny, just what Wyatt had ordered. He waited for a reaction within him, even a little trickle of curiosity, but the woman stuck on his mind was smaller, lighter, tough as nails, yet soft as silk.

And he could still taste her kiss.

With an apologetic smile, he headed for the locker room, where he put his skis away for the night. On the bench opposite his locker sat another woman, late thirties, shiny blond hair, perfect makeup, fancy diamonds dangling off her ears. She wore tight black ski pants and an even tighter sunshine-yellow V-neck sweater that screamed "woman on the prowl."

"Do you work here?" she asked in a soft, husky voice, running her fingers over her deep-plunging neckline.

"No." Logan stifled his impatience with the ritual flirtation dance and wondered what the hell his problem was. He sat on the bench to remove his ski boots. "Just visiting."

"Oh. Me, too. Actually, I own the place."

"Really?" He dropped one boot into the locker. "Because I met another owner yesterday on the slopes."

"Lily Rose." The woman laughed. "My niece. She owns a bigger piece than me. Which means *she* has to do all the work while I get to come and go as I please." She smiled. "Are you having a nice time?"

He didn't have to think about it, which surprised him. "Very."

"The snow is so amazing here, isn't it? I'm used to skiing back east on ice. This place spoils me."

Making an agreeing noise, he removed his other boot.

"Tomorrow is supposed to be gorgeous. Sun and fun on the Sierras."

He put that boot on the floor of the locker, as well, and smiled absently.

"Wow. You have a great smile." She thrust out a hand. "I'm Debbie, by the way."

"Logan." He shook the hand she offered and looked into her hungry eyes…still nothing.

"I hope I see you around, Logan. Maybe in the bar, or the hot tub…" With a last, very direct smile, she patted his shoulder and sashayed out of the locker area.

Logan sighed at himself and headed down the stone staircase toward his room. He figured he'd take a shower and then go eat. And then take the evening from there.

His room was small but as warm and inviting as the rest of the resort. The walls, painted a soft buttery color, featured framed photographs of the Tahoe area from the late 1800s and early 1900s. The mismatched antique dresser and chair seemed like a perfect fit for the four-poster bed and its patchwork quilt.

He stripped out of his ski gear and took a long, hot shower, letting the water beat on his back while his mind wandered…right to Lily.

Unlike Logan, she didn't have a week off. She wasn't suddenly…lonely. *Damn it*. He got dressed and went back upstairs, determined to mingle. To be excited at the prospect of being on his own again. Eating alone in the cafeteria, smiling at strangers, suddenly held little appeal, however, so he headed into the bar, thinking a beer might settle this odd restlessness.

The bar was done up like an old western saloon, complete with swinging double wood doors, bar stools made from saddles and tables that were shellacked wooden telephone spindles turned on their ends. The place was nearly full, and laughter and talk rang out in pleasant tones as he walked in.

At home, he and the members of his team often met at Moody's after an incredibly tough shift, needing to unwind. Logan could walk into that bar any day of the week and come across friends to hang out with. He hadn't gotten that same level of intimacy last night when he'd wandered through here; this bar had a different energy altogether. It was edgier, louder—more about fun—but still a welcoming place.

Moving through the crowd, he took a seat on a bar stool. There were two women bartending, both with their backs to him. The closest one was petite in size and wore a black beanie, black leggings on her tight, toned legs, a black silky thermal top that came to her thighs and a white apron, somehow managing to make the simple undergarments look fashionable. When she turned to get his order, a smile split her face.

He felt the same silly thing happen to him. "Lily Rose."

5

"WHAT DID I TELL YOU ABOUT my middle name?" There was a teasing lilt in those whiskey-colored eyes as Lily spoke. "Have you been enjoying yourself?"

"More so now." Reaching out, Logan put his hand over hers and felt the icy cold of her skin sing along his. "Holy smokes."

"I know. I'm a Popsicle. I just got in a few minutes ago."

He entwined her fingers in his and gave a little squeeze, trying to give her some of his warmth. She had short, unpainted fingernails that looked as if maybe she sometimes chewed them, and a silver heart ring on her right thumb, which he glided a finger over. He felt a little tremor go through her body, but didn't flatter himself. The woman was frozen solid. "Lily, you need a hot shower. How's your knee?"

"I haven't had a chance to look at it today."

"And I thought *I* was dedicated."

She laughed again, a soft, musical sound that seemed to wrap around him. "I'm glad to see you here. I figured I scared you off good yesterday, what with all the drama."

"Nah." Odd how his restlessness had vanished.

Granted, being with this woman wasn't exactly a leisurely vacation, but he thought that what they could
share for the next few days might be a lot better. "You
should come live a day in my life sometime. I'm not
talking just ski-slope opera drama, either. We face a
wider variety of stupidity."

Her smile was slow and sexy. "You're not scaring
me off."

"I wasn't trying to. So why are you working the
bar?"

"Matt's running late."

"Matt?"

"Remember Sara?"

"The sister worried about you stealing another
Jeep?"

"That's the one. Matt's her husband. He's the bartender tonight, I'm just filling in until he gets here."

"You have a big family. I met your aunt Debbie."

"Ah." She looked him over. "I see she let you go
without sinking her teeth into you. She must be losing her touch."

"Maybe I wasn't interested."

She shrugged, but he would have sworn that his
answer pleased her. Still, she backed up, spread out
her white apron and bowed. "What can I get you
tonight?"

If she only knew. "Whatcha got?"

"A little of everything. Hot, cold, spicy, sweet…
name your poison."

"Hmm." He found himself smiling, feeling totally
alive. And incredibly, arousingly aware. "How about
something slow, with a kick."

Her eyes darkened just a little. "Are we still talking drinks?"

"That, too."

A variety of emotions crossed her face. Excitement. Thrill. Nerves. The combination was wickedly stimulating.

Her gaze dropped to his mouth while she dragged her lower lip between her teeth. He'd bet his last buck she was thinking about their kiss.

Good. That made two of them.

"Something slow with a kick…" She turned away to survey all the possibilities.

He snagged her wrist, waiting until she looked at him. Her hand was still icy, but now her lips were chattering, too. He'd been outside all day too many times to miss the signs. She was badly chilled.

"No," she said, and pulled free.

"I didn't say anything."

"You were going to tell me to go get warm, and you'll help out while I do."

"It's not a bad plan."

"Except…"

"You're not a woman who likes needing help?"

"No. But thank you," she added softly. "It's sweet. You're sweet."

"What I'm thinking about is quite probably the furthest thing from sweet you've ever seen. Do you want to know what I'm thinking?"

She stared at him, shivered hard. "Yes."

He had to laugh. No woman he'd ever known would have said yes. "I'm thinking of all the ways I can warm you up." He leaned forward. "With—"

She put a finger to his lips. "You're warming me up already. You have a way of looking at me, Logan White."

"Do I?"

"Like you want to gobble me up."

"Does that frighten you?"

"Nothing frightens me."

Someone down the bar gestured for a refill, and she smiled her apology and moved toward them. A lanky guy with a head of dark curls made his way behind the bar and gave her a big bear hug with a smacking kiss right on the lips.

Matt, Logan assumed.

Lily stripped out of her apron and a moment later came to Logan's side with two whiskey shots. She sat down next to him, picked up her glass and lifted it in a toast. "To warmth on a snowy winter's eve."

He lifted his glass, too, and touched it to hers. "To being warm together on a winter's eve."

Her lips curved. "Even better."

He agreed. And though he rarely drank anything harder than a beer, he took the shot.

She did the same, then swiped her mouth with her arm and smiled. "That should help."

"Yeah, so would—"

"Lily Rose." A woman who looked remarkably like Lily came up to them. She had Lily's brown, bouncy long curls, Lily's whiskey eyes, though not as happy, and Lily's face, only at least ten years older. Her mouth tightened at the shot glass in Lily's hand. "I need a moment."

"Now's bad."

"*Please*."

Logan could tell the word, uttered sincerely, surprised Lily, and she nodded. "All right. Excuse me," she said to him.

He watched her follow her sister out of the bar, limping fairly steadily on that knee as she went. He set a ten-dollar bill on the bar to pay for the two whiskeys and then followed the two women, not exactly sure why he felt so dead set on getting Lily warmed up and fed. *Old habits,* he thought—that same protective instinct that hundreds of SAR call-outs had honed—but the knowledge didn't stop him. He figured it had been way too long since anyone had protected Lily.

Lily and her sister stood off in a dim corner of the hallway.

"For God's sake, Lily Rose! You can't drink with the guests! It's bad enough people are talking about the missing out-of-bounds signs, now they'll worry about the wild woman who runs this place."

"People are not talking."

"Yes, they are. You shouldn't be behind that bar, you have a crew. Honestly, if you can't manage this thing, I told you I could step in, but you never ask for help."

"Hold on." Lily let out a low laugh. "I don't need your help."

"I beg to differ."

"Look, I'm killing myself to manage this resort, and I'm doing a damn fine job of it. If you don't think so, you can just bite me."

"*Bite me?* Is that the mature response here?"

"It's an honest one."

"You were drinking. With a *guest*."

"Well, clearly, I'm going to hell."

"Lily Rose—"

Logan vowed never to tease her with the name Rose again.

Lily leaned into Gwyneth. "I don't have to explain myself but I'm going to because I'm feeling charitable. I've never had a drink with a guest before."

"Really? How about that time you were found on the floor of the bar, nuzzling directly from the beer on tap? You weren't alone."

"I was *sixteen*. And okay, yes, I was with the daughter of a guest, but she was sixteen, too. I paid for that mistake, you know I did. Grandpa nearly killed me. And Grandma made me clean all the toilets and showers in the inn, daily, for my entire sophomore year."

"I'm just saying."

Lily rubbed her face. "Gwyneth, I've had a long day. I'm cold and wet. I'm going to my room to shower."

"And then?"

"Whatever strikes my fancy."

"I worry about you, Lily."

"No, you worry about Bay Moon, and how long it'll take me to screw up. I'm not going to. Get used to that."

"Is that what you think? That I'm just watching for you to screw up? My God, Lily. Really?"

Lily rubbed her temples. "I'm too tired for this. Good night, Gwyneth."

"Good night." Gwyneth sighed. "Just…be careful, will you?"

"Always." They both turned to go their separate ways.

Logan knew the exact moment Lily saw him because she lifted a brow. "Logan. This is my sister, Gwyneth."

Gwyneth shook his hand while giving him the eagle eye. "How long are you staying with us?"

"The rest of the week."

"By yourself?"

"Gwyneth—" Lily said warningly.

"Yes," Logan answered. "I'm by myself, on vacation."

"Which we already messed up yesterday," Lily said. "When he jumped in and helped me on patrol. By the way, we're comping you one of your days," she told him. "And some entertainment stuff, too, like snowmobile riding, maybe ice skating...whatever you want."

"That's not necessary."

"Yes," she said. "It is."

So formal suddenly, and so distant. He wondered what had happened. Had it been her sister hammering at her? No, she didn't seem the type to care what anyone else thought.

She moved away from Gwyneth and he walked with her. "Just two sisters, right?" he asked in a low voice.

"Yes. Thankfully." And as she had from her sister, she turned away. "I'll see you, Logan."

"Count on it." He watched her go, wondering how to reach her again, or if he even wanted to.

But he knew he did.

Very much.

LILY DIDN'T SEE LOGAN AGAIN that night. After her shower, Aunt Debbie showed up in her room with a gift of gorgeous silver-and-crystal earrings, regaling her with her New York life and how great it had been over the past year.

Then there'd been a problem with the plumbing in the ski shop's employee bathroom, and after that, a computer crash. Since their computer guy was a high school techno-head in town—also the baby brother of their cafeteria chef—who'd gotten himself arrested for joyriding in his aunt's car just last week and no longer had access to a vehicle, Lily had to go get him.

By the time all the fires were put out, it was past midnight. The bar was still hopping, but Logan wasn't in it. Nor was he in the cafeteria or the open lodge area or the hot tub. She couldn't blame him—it'd been hours since he'd said he'd see her.

But disappointment flooded her. Once again, the lodge had taken over her life, keeping her from something she'd wanted. *Someone* she'd wanted.

With a sigh for what might have been, and then another for her easy, carefree life of old, she dragged herself off to bed.

6

THE NEXT DAY DAWNED BRILLIANT, with a sky so bright and blue that Lily needed sunglasses just to look at it. She loved mornings like this, with the air lung-searingly crisp and clean. She stood on the outside deck of the cafeteria, overlooking the mountain. Unfortunately the news she was getting from her chef was seriously compromising her enjoyment of the morning.

Carl stood there hovering while she looked over the menus for the week, his skinny arms wrapped around his skinnier body. "I don't know what happened," he said. "I'm telling you, I always get the breads delivered like clockwork. But they swear you called them and told them no deliveries this week. Why did you do that?"

Aunt Debbie was kicking back against the railing of the deck, looking smug at not having any responsibilities. She sipped her coffee and eyed Carl speculatively.

"I didn't cancel a delivery." Lily was baffled, but also irritated. People weren't going to be happy eating hamburgers without buns, chili without bread bowls, breakfast without toast....

"And why the hell do we always have to have our morning meeting outside?" he grumbled, shivering.

"Because she's got ice in her veins," Debbie said cheerfully.

"Do you mind?" Lily asked. "We're having a meeting here."

"Sorry." She didn't look it.

Carl shivered again. Though he hated the winters, he'd been working at Bay Moon for ten years, ever since he'd graduated high school. He'd started out cleaning tables and had talked his way into cooking. Tall, dark-haired and scrawny, he'd turned out to be a god in the kitchen, a miraculous find who could whip up anything under the sun, and often did, just for fun. His genius with food made her overlook his complaints about the winter, the snow and the general misery that this season caused him.

It boggled Lily's mind that anyone would willingly go into a kitchen and cook and call it fun, but over and over again their guests wrote entire fan letters devoted to the talents of this one man. As for the outdoor meetings, Carl and her grandmother had always had their meetings outside, and Lily wasn't going to break with tradition. She'd once taken pity on him and had an indoor meeting only to have him mope around for the entire shift, talking about how "some people" didn't respect the past.

"It's so cold, my parts are frozen," he complained.

Lily's grandma had loved him, and so did she. Every long, scrawny, grumpy inch of him. "Chefs don't whine," she said absently, looking over his menu.

"They do when it's twenty-five degrees outside. Jeez, Lil, have a heart."

Debbie looked amused.

"Stand in the sun." Lily whipped out her cell and called the distributor. Damn if they didn't swear she'd canceled. Irate but relatively calm, she spoke to the supervisor. And got nowhere. She disconnected. "You're going to have to get creative without bread until tomorrow."

Lips blue, he shrugged. "Fine. Just make sure no one screws with tomorrow's delivery."

"Oh, I plan to."

He glanced longingly inside. "Look, I have the heater on in the kitchen, all nice and toasty-like. You come in and I'll make you up my egg special. With the ham in it, just how you like it. No toast though. My boss, see, she screwed up my order."

"Stop it, I didn't screw up anything." But someone had, and she'd find out who, too.

She lifted her gaze and scanned the horizon. From this strategic spot, guests could take in the rocky, craggy Sierras, dipped in white and lined with ribbons of frosted pines as far as the eye could see. For once, however, she felt too disgruntled to enjoy the great view. Who would pull such a stupid, disruptive stunt?

"I'd love the special, but you'll have to send it to my office." With a sigh, she passed back the menu with an approving nod. "I'll be with your brother, who right now is dealing with our computers and Sara."

"*Oy.*"

"Yeah. Make that a double."

"I'll come to the kitchen for the special," Debbie said.

Lily followed them, scanning the busy tables as she walked through the cafeteria. She told herself she was checking to make sure everyone looked happy, but she was really looking for a dark, wavy mane of hair and matching eyes, a smile that never failed to render her stupid and a body that she could happily look at for the rest of his stay.

But Logan White wasn't there. Probably wasn't a morning person, or maybe he'd already hit the slopes. She didn't know, and it shouldn't matter, but as she moved through the cafeteria into the rest of the lodge, she kept a vigil, finally having to admit defeat.

The computer issue took the entire morning, hours made slightly more livable because Carl kept his word and sent her food. After that, she had a shift to cover in the ski shop because someone had called in sick. *Sick.* Even she knew better than that. The day after a snowfall, with fresh powder on the hills, she always lost twenty percent of her employees to the "powder flu." She couldn't really blame them, she'd have done the same thing.

If she hadn't owned the place, damn it. She wanted to be out there, too! Every time she passed a window, she slowed down, mentally pressing her nose to the glass, pathetic and yearning.

Unfortunately the rest of the day went by without a single chance to get out. That really ate at her because in no time at all, the season would be over and she'd be forced to get her adrenaline fix in other ways, such as on her mountain bike, which, while fun, wasn't the same.

By evening, she still sat at her desk, staring sightlessly at the stacks of work yet to be done, always to be done, and rubbed her temples. For so much of this past year she'd worked night and day like this. It was killing her, absolutely killing her. She needed some time, needed to rejuvenate her spirit. True, she got outside a lot, and on the slopes she loved so much. But much of that time was spent with one ear cocked on the radio, patrolling or fielding calls from her sisters. No just-Lily time.

Her sisters didn't seem to need that.

Yet another example of how she must be an alien baby that her parents had found on their porch one morning twenty-five years ago.

When her stomach growled, it was a reason to wander through the cafeteria. Again, she wondered what Logan was doing. Was he wandering the unique shops and galleries in town? Out with someone he'd met today on the slopes? He'd have had no trouble meeting a woman interested in him. Hell, any woman with a pulse would be interested in him. That gorgeous face and even more magnificent body, topped with an intriguingly sharp mind and wit, not to mention the way he kissed—

Her walkie-talkie rang out and she wished it could be Danny with an emergency on the slopes that she could go help with. Pitiful, wishing for an emergency just to get out, but since the slopes were closed for the day, the odds weren't good.

"I'm going to be thirty minutes late for my shift," Matt said in a rush.

"But your shift starts—" she glanced down at her watch "—now."

"I know. Sorry. Can you cover me?"

"Yeah, yeah." She clicked off and headed toward the bar. She knew Matt was currently working two jobs to pay for a surprise for Sara—his wife and Lily's sister—an addition to their small log-cabin house on the hill above town. He and Sara loved the location, but the house only had one bedroom and bath, and with Sara seven and a half months pregnant and grumpy to boot, they had definitely outgrown their starter home.

Lily's sister had no idea why Matt had been putting in such brutal hours, but the surprise would definitely make her easier to live with, and Lily was looking forward to that phenomenon greatly.

They had a live band in the bar tonight, playing eighties covers and rocking the house. The small crowd was mostly dressed in the winter gear she fondly referred to as "Sierra Casual," meaning jeans and fleece—except Debbie, who was dressed to the nines. There was a comfortable air about the place she'd purposely cultivated. People felt at home here, and because they did, the bar was a steady and important source of income for the resort.

As she took Matt's shift serving the guests, she kept one eye on the door, watching new arrivals, hoping for only one.

Didn't happen.

No biggie, she told herself. She'd been disappointed before, many times. At least tonight she wore jeans and a sweater and wasn't cold, wet and hungry. Unfortunately her knee was killing her, and so was her neck, both compliments of the other day's crash. Her shoulders hurt, too, and she thought maybe she'd make a hot-tub stop later before heading off to bed.

"Lily."

She turned from the margaritas she was mixing and faced Sara. Unlike Gwyneth, Sara did not resent Lily for inheriting the whole family pie. And unlike Gwyneth, she actually *liked* peace in the family, meaning she was often the one running back and forth soothing the feathers that Lily and Gwyneth ruffled without even trying. But she'd given up most of the family meddling and soothing to do her own, with Matt.

Matt was a happy-go-lucky kind of guy who enjoyed people, meaning he was perfectly suited for bartending at Bay Moon. That the hapless cutie had snagged the beautiful but high-maintenance Sara still had heads shaking in bafflement all around town, but fact was fact, and he really did love her. More shocking, she loved him back, ridiculously. He always put a smile on her face and softened her edges, which made Matt an absolute hero in Lily's eyes.

"I need to talk to you," Sara said. "It's bad."

Oh, boy. Lily racked her brain and could think of nothing she'd done that would be considered a problem, but Sara's mind worked in mysterious ways. Still, Lily absolutely did not want to do this in the bar—whatever *this* might be—and tried to direct Sara outside. They made it as far as the double swinging saloon doors.

"I can't believe you're covering for Matt again." Sara didn't look mad, which was a huge relief for

Lily, but the misery in her sister's eyes made the relief short-lived.

"It was a last-minute thing," Lily said, having promised Matt she wouldn't give away the surprise.

Sara nodded, rubbing the ever-increasing bump beneath her sweater. "I think he's lying to me."

"Why don't you sit down and take a load off. I'll make you a hot chocolate."

"I don't want to sit down. Did you hear me? I think my husband is *lying* to me."

"I just think for the sake of this—" Lily pointed to the baby "—you should sit down."

"It's not a *this*." Sara's eyes filled. "It's a b-b-baby, and maybe he doesn't want it anymore. Maybe it's me and how fat I've become!"

"No, it's not—"

"Then what's keeping him lately? Where the hell is he? Oh, my God." She clapped her hands over her mouth. "He's changed his mind about me. That's it, isn't it?"

Matt had warned her that Sara's mood swings were bordering on manic, and Lily glanced at the door, wondering how long he'd be. "He probably just got held up on the road. Listen, Sara, I really have to serve—"

"It's because I'm cranky, right?"

"Uh…"

"Well, you'd be cranky too if you'd gained enough weight that your scale groaned when you got on it. If it could talk, it'd say, 'One at a time, please!'"

"Sara—"

"What if you knew that in six weeks you had to

pass a basketball out your vagina? Huh? Wouldn't you feel entitled to a few emotional breakdowns?"

Lily scrunched up her eyes but, nope, no good, the image of a basketball coming out of a vagina stuck.

"Do I look *that* fat?" Sara asked miserably.

Trick question. Lily knew the rules: never answer the trick questions. Matt had taught her that one himself.

"If he's cheating on me, I'm going to castrate him." Sara looked serious. "Slowly. That'll make us even."

Lily looked over Sara's shoulder at Matt, who'd just come down the hallway and had gone very still and a bit pale. Behind him, Logan came along, looking tall, dark and yummy, and for a moment Lily lost her concentration because her body did a happy-hormone dance.

"You know where he is," Sara said to Lily, oblivious. "I can tell when you're lying. Remember that July Fourth when you blew up my toilet with the illegal fireworks you bought from a buddy? You said God was telling me to stop spending so much time in the bathroom, but I knew it was you."

"That was never proven."

"Where is he, Lily?"

Matt shot Lily his puppy-dog look and silently begged her not to tell where he'd been. She took one last peek at Logan and then forced her gaze off him before she did something stupid. Like drool. Instead, she rubbed her aching neck. "I don't know. But he doesn't think you're fat and he wants the baby. He's crazy about you."

That much was the utter, baffling truth at least. In her life, there'd been a lot of dissent. Her parents had traveled a lot for their jobs, and when they had been in the same house for any amount of time, they'd fought. Her grandparents had never greeted a day without a bicker.

As a result, she and her sisters had developed relationships based on their own bickering hierarchy, with Lily at the bottom, of course. But then Matt had come into Sara's life and Lily had witnessed a deeper bond than she'd ever imagined could exist. Matt would do anything for Sara, anything. "You know he loves you. He's such a sap."

Matt lifted an eyebrow. *Sap?*

Revenge made her smile. "You've got him wrapped around your little pinkie. You know it."

Sara sniffed. "You only think that because you're relationship challenged. You don't understand."

Hard to dispute the truth. Relationships, like love, gave her the hives. But she wouldn't mind a few days of mutual lust. With the man who was standing next to Matt, watching her every move with that quiet intensity that made her want to dive at him.

Sara sighed and held the big lump of her belly, looking pale.

"Let's sit down," Lily tried again. "I'll rub your back."

"Don't worry, I'm not going into labor. I'm not *ever* going into labor. I'm going to be pregnant forever."

"Whatever you say," Lily soothed, trying to pull Sara toward a table. "You still need to sit down. Matt'll be here any second, so—" She'd been about to suggest Sara wipe away the mascara dripping down her cheeks or comb her ratty hair, but Matt came forward and wrapped his arms around his wife.

"Hey, baby," he said, and hugged her unresponsive form. He went to kiss her mouth but she gave him a cheek. "Sorry I'm late."

Sara stared at him. "Does your new girlfriend wear perfume that smells like a cedar chest?"

"Uh…"

"Because you smell like a cedar chest, Matt."

"Yeah, that's my fault," Lily said quickly.

"Really? How is that?" Sara asked.

Yes, Lily, how was that? "Well…" Her mind raced around the fact that Matt's second job was at the lumber mill. "He picked up some supplies for me." *Brilliant*, she thought. A good excuse and more revenge at the same time. "For that new cabinet and shelves I need in my office." She smiled sweetly at Matt, who was looking a little strained. "I can't wait to see what you're going to build me."

"I can't believe you're selfish enough to demand new shelves now, when *I* need him," Sara said, shocked.

"That's me, selfish queen bee."

Matt opened his mouth but Sara melted against him. "Oh, Matt." Her eyes were suspiciously shiny. "Really? You're sweet enough to build my sister some shelves?"

"Uh…yes. Yes, I am."

"Oh, honey." Sara threw her arms around his neck and sobbed. "I'm so sorry. I'm losing my mind."

Lily had to give Matt kudos for not pointing out that yes, Sara *was* losing her mind. Instead, he just

held her tight and said, "I love you" and then laughed
when Sara dragged him out of the bar, murmuring
something about her out-of-control hormones.

"Hey!" Lily called after them. "Hey, you come
back here, you're on duty!"

Matt glanced back at her. "Give me a few more
minutes?"

"Damn it."

Logan pushed away from where he'd been holding up the wall and came toward her. "I hope he ap-
preciates you."

"Oh, he will. The whole time he's building me
new shelves."

He took her hand, stroked a thumb over her
knuckles, and everything within her tightened.

He looked her over, from her favorite pair of faded
jeans to her forest-green cashmere hoodie sweater
and matching beanie that she'd stuffed her wild, out-
of-control hair into. She'd dressed at the crack of
dawn in a hurry, more for comfort than style, but
watching him take her in, seeing his eyes heat, suddenly she felt feminine. Even pretty.

Then a slow sexy smile curved his lips and her
body, already alert, quivered. "I thought about you
today."

"Did you?"

"Oh, yeah."

And just like that, she didn't feel so sore and tired
anymore.

He tugged her just a little closer, blocking her
view of the bar with his broad shoulders. "How was
your day?"

"That's my line to you."

"I skied. It was amazing. No emergencies today, though." Reaching up, he stroked away a long strand of hair poking out of her beanie and into her eye. "You didn't get out?"

"Too busy." Still was. Sasha, the other bartender, was sending her frantic help-me glances. "In fact, I've got to go," she said very reluctantly.

"That's too bad."

She looked into his dark eyes and sighed. He didn't know the half of it. "I'll buy you a drink," she said. "What would you like?"

His free hand came up, his fingers dancing over the side of her neck, lightly probing right over her sore muscles. "Are you hurting?"

The touch sent little shock waves through her system. "Just a little kink."

He massaged it, applying a pressure so gentle that she wanted to drop into a puddle on the floor. "Oh, my God."

"Good?"

"Extremely." She bit back her moan and locked her knees to avoid falling to the floor. "Are you hungry?"

Cocking his head, he studied her with that dark, dark gaze. "You're awfully good at that. Deflecting the pampering."

"It's my job."

"I don't want to be your job."

"No?"

"It should be your turn for a little pampering."

She laughed. "Not in my job description, unfortunately. I really do need to go."

He caught her hand when she would have moved toward the bar. "Two days ago you made me an honorary member of your staff."

"I did."

"Maybe you could do the same right now."

Her breath caught. "What job would you like?"

"You."

The temperature in the room shot up, and Lily looked him over. For two nights, he'd played heavily in her fantasies. She'd already decided it'd been too long since she'd indulged in a nice—or not-so-nice—hot fling. "Have at it."

His answering smile was the sexiest, wickedest thing she'd ever seen and nearly melted her bones. She wished, just for a moment, for her old, uncomplicated life.

"I'm just afraid it'll have to be later. I have to get to the bar."

When he followed her, sitting at one of the tables as she went behind the bar and began working, she couldn't help feeling pleased. Work was a heck of a lot more fun when she had a great view. She brought him a beer as soon as she and Sasha caught up with the rush.

He tugged her down next to him, and she smiled. "Are you tired of being alone on vacation?"

"I'm not often by myself. I'm doing fine."

"Search and rescue keeps you pretty busy, I imagine."

"I thought so. Until I saw you. I think you're busier."

She laughed. "Not because I want to be, trust me. Tell me about your work. It sounds more interesting. You fly your own helicopter?"

"I own it with a partner. Wyatt and I both have other jobs, as well. He flies traffic reporters and I fly people with too much money to meetings with other people with too much money. It pays the bills," he said with a shrug.

"It's a lot nicer than paying them from behind a desk. How did you get into all this?"

"Coast guard. My father and both my brothers are military, too."

She smiled. "So you live in quite the testosterone world."

"Guess so."

"And yet by the very nature of what you do, you're there for others, saving them. Nurturing."

He tipped his beer to his lips and took a pull.

She read the irritation in his expression and laughed. "Oh, sorry. I know a guy doesn't want to hear the word *nurturing* in connection with his character. Don't worry, Logan, what you do is incredibly dangerous and also sexy as hell."

He ran a finger over the wet label on his beer. "Same goes." He met her gaze then, hot and breathtaking.

With a low laugh, she stood up. "I've got to get back."

He stood, too, and took her hand, squeezing it gently until she looked at him. "I'd like to see you later."

There was nothing she'd like more. Maybe she'd been extra careful this year to fit the mold of resort manager and owner, too much so, but she needed something for herself. Never shy, she smiled. "Later sounds good."

"Where do I find you?"

She looked at him for a long moment, her engine revving. "Down that stone hallway are the employee offices. Past that is another wing. My apartment is the second door on the right."

He looked into her eyes, and when he didn't say anything, she wondered if she'd jumped the gun. Maybe he hadn't intended for them to rendezvous tonight at all. Or maybe he didn't like aggressive women—

"Later seems too far away, but I'll live," he said softly and, with one last dance of his fingers over her throat, let go of her hand. "Tonight, then."

God, she hoped so. Her entire body hoped so.

7

An hour and a half later, Logan made his way through the common room. The fire was low but still crackling and popping. People milled around here and there: a few guys talking in a corner, a couple holding hands, another man and a woman—Lily's aunt in fact—flirting on the couch in the late, quiet night.

He hadn't expected to still be awake himself after three long, hard, exciting days on the slopes, but that had been before Lily had leveled him with her whiskey eyes and given him directions to her room.

At the startlingly open invitation, he'd been floored, flattered and, even now, aroused.

Three days into his weeklong vacation and he was enjoying himself more than he'd imagined possible, something he'd admitted to Wyatt before dinner when Wyatt had called to make sure he was having fun.

"You get yourself a ski bunny yet?" had been the first thing out of Wyatt's mouth.

"The skiing's good, thanks for asking."

"Yeah. Good. Just tell me this…is she hot?"

Sizzling. "'Bye, Wyatt."

With anticipation humming through him, he made his way down the darkened hallway of the employee offices and into a separate wing, where he came to a stop at the second door on the right.

He knocked, and when the door opened, Lily stood there looking at him with a surprise she couldn't quite hide.

Had she thought he wouldn't show? "Hey," he said softly. "Too late?"

"No." She let out a slow smile. "Not too late at all."

Yeah, she'd definitely thought he wouldn't show. Had there been that many broken promises, that many disappointments?

And why did that tug on the heart he hadn't intended to engage?

She stepped back and made room for him to come in, then made a sound of frustration when her phone rang. "Excuse me."

Her living room was small but comfy-looking, with a pillow-filled couch in front of a fireplace. There were pictures on the walls, landscapes of the Sierras and Lake Tahoe and some other intriguing vistas he didn't recognize. She had a small kitchen off to the side, done in bold red and white, and then another door.

Her bedroom?

Phone to her ear, Lily paced in front of the fireplace. "Yes, Gwyneth, I bolted the bear box." She listened a moment. "Well, wasn't that nice of Aunt Debbie to worry about me doing my job. Look, do us both a favor and go to sleep." She clicked the phone off and drew a deep breath.

Seemed his wild ski bunny was tense, very tense. And not such a wild ski bunny at all. "Nice accommodations," he said, wanting to see a smile back on her face.

"Thanks." She looked around. "I keep thinking I'll buy my own place in town but I just love to be on site. I'm the only one who lives here full-time, since my grandma died last year."

His gaze cut to hers, and he didn't miss the quick stab of pain there. "You were close?"

"Very close— Damn it." She went to the kitchen counter and picked up her beeping pager. Reading the display, she put a hand to her neck and sighed.

"Trouble?"

"No." She set the pager down and visibly shrugged it off. "How about your family? You didn't mention your mom. You close?"

"She left us when we were fairly young." He lifted a shoulder. "I don't remember her."

She studied him for a long, considering moment. "And as the oldest, you probably did a lot of the raising of your brothers."

"Enough that even now they enjoy calling me *Mom* just to listen to me growl."

She smiled, then turned from him and walked over to the fireplace. Crouching down, she took a stack of sticks from a pile and began to crisscross them inside the stone hearth. She still wore the hip-hugging jeans that revealed an extremely nice ass, her wipe apron, that soft, fuzzy forest-green hooded sweater that just barely met the denim and the matching beanie that was squashed down on her head, revealing long bangs in the front and a braid in the back. Casual. Sweet, even. But his reaction had nothing to do with sweet.

She lit a match, waited until the sticks caught, then added a log on top. Standing, she faced him again, fingers linked together. "Did you want a drink?"

"No, thanks." He noted she was rubbing her neck again. "Are you ready, Lily?"

"For…?"

On the corner of the stone mantel sat a basket, its contents catching his attention—not the green toenail polish or the *People* magazine, but the body lotion. Scooping it up in his hand, he held it out.

Lily stared at the lotion, then lifted her gaze to his.

"I'll start with that kink in your neck," he said.

The pulse at the base of her throat leaped. "And finish with…?"

He looked right into her eyes. "Whatever you want."

Yum, said Lily's body. *Whoa*, said her mind, but only for a moment, and even then she chose to shove it to the background. Whatever she wanted? He'd better be prepared because suddenly she wanted a whole hell of a lot, especially if he kept looking at her like that.

"You work so hard," he said. "And tonight—"cupping her face, he tilted it up, running his thumb over her lower lip, making it tremble "—you seemed sad."

"I wasn't." But she had been. Damn it, she *had* been sad and restless and lonely for reasons she couldn't put her finger on, and it scared her that he'd seen it.

"You put so much of yourself into this place. Don't let anyone take that from you, Lily. Not your sisters, not anyone."

After only a few days, he'd seen. He'd understood. She tried to swallow the lump in her throat, but she couldn't so she stepped back and turned away because this wasn't going to be the easy, wild, forgettable evening she'd wanted. "This is a mistake."

"Really? Then we'll have to make it count." He tugged her around, and then his mouth was on hers, devouring, sending her into frenzy-mode with one stroke of his greedy tongue.

Long before she was done, he pulled back and, still facing her, began kneading her shoulders, not even needing the lotion, showing the same talent with which he'd just kissed her stupid. By the time he dug in with his thumbs, she was putty in his hands, but she locked her knees. "Let's spell this out."

"Spell what out?"

"Exactly what we're doing."

"Which is…?"

"I thought it'd be sex."

He let out a low, husky laugh. "Okay."

She tilted her head up to see him. "That's all this is? Nothing else?"

His eyes told her the truth. He wanted more. "Lily—"

"Look, that's all I've got." And though she'd told him she was fearless, that was one big, fat lie. This scared her. He scared her. "You're only here for a few more nights so just be straight with me. No strings attached is what I'm offering. Simple. Now you say yes or no."

"That sounds—"

"Honest." She unzipped her hoodie sweater and

tossed it to the couch, leaving her clad only in a snug, thin tank. She heard his abrupt intake of breath and figured the pale silk had snagged his attention. Maybe he'd say yes.

"Lily—"

"Yes or no, Logan."

"I have no doubt we can make it count," he assured her in a voice that had her every sensual nerve ending doing a twitchy dance.

"Yes or no?"

"Yes."

She nearly staggered at the heat in his eyes. Maybe she *had* been sad earlier, stinging from the pressure she put on herself, including constantly proving that she was worthy of the responsibility she shouldered. Damn it, she deserved this, and knowing it, she took a step toward him.

Her pager went off yet again, but before she could react, Logan walked into the kitchen and picked it up from the counter. He opened her freezer and set it on the top shelf, next to a tray of ice cubes. Next he took the telephone off the hook. Then he looked at her, all tough and edgy and just enough of a stranger to boost her heart rate. "How's that?"

"Good." She loved the take-charge, dare-me expression on his face, and a shiver raced down her spine—one that had nothing to do with the cold, dark night and everything to do with the man standing in front of her.

When he opened his arms, she walked right into them. Kissing him was like waking up from a long sleep, slow and gentle at first, which lasted exactly until he slid his hand up and down her back, then beneath her tank top to touch bare skin. It was electrifying, and letting out a low moan, she leaned into him as the heat rose inside her.

It pumped off him, as well, and then it went wild and just a little rough, which was perfect for her because she didn't want to think, she just wanted to feel. And feeling Logan, tough and hard against her, his muscles taut and quivering, went a long way toward ensuring that she wouldn't have to think at all.

His arm hooked around her, lifted her right off the ground, giving her a foolish little thrill at the easy strength of him. His mouth was hot, his tongue insistent, the shock of it sending licks of flame throughout her entire body so that she vibrated. He wanted her. Not the resort owner, or even the wild woman she had a rep for, he just wanted...*her*.

My God, she thought with a low moan, that was so damn arousing. "Bedroom."

But he held her there, high against him. He kept kissing her jaw, her throat, her shoulders, then her mouth again, and frustrated, she tried to drag him off to her bed to devour him back.

"Slow down," he murmured, his hands sliding up her spine, beneath her shirt, then back down, cupping her bottom in his hands, squeezing. "What's your hurry?"

What was her hurry? She needed him, damn it. Needed the oblivion she knew he could give her, *now, now, now*. Impatient, she yanked his shirt free of his jeans, then ran her hands inside, up his belly, over his pecs.

He shivered. "God, Lily."

"I know. *More.*" To show him, she nibbled her way to his ear, bit down on the lobe hard enough to make him hiss, then soothed the nip with her tongue, all while trying to tug off his long-sleeved T-shirt.

He lifted his arms to oblige her, smiling roughly against her skin when she found another T-shirt beneath and groaned.

"Why are you wearing so many clothes?" she demanded.

"I don't know, I won't next time."

When she got him down to bare skin, she couldn't take her eyes or hands off his perfectly formed torso. "You're so beautiful."

He grabbed her face, holding her still for a hot, long kiss that made her yearn and burn all the more. Hell, she'd really thought to keep this light, easy, but there was nothing light or easy about how he drew her in and held her there, quivering, hungry, desperate. Entwining her arms around his neck, she kissed him back and felt herself slide into him, and then even a little deeper. She could feel him taut and hard against her, just as hungry and desperate as she, and it nearly made her pull back so that she could get her bearings and make sure he remembered this was supposed to be just scratching an itch.

But his eyes were dark, so dark, and his mouth was wet from hers. His breathing was uneven. Harsh. But with a tenderness she hadn't imagined such a big, tough guy could possess, he stroked his thumb over her still-damp lower lip and let out a shuddery sigh.

And her heart sighed, too.

Their eyes met, held, and the silence spoke volumes. This was it. Tonight. *Now.*

She wanted him. She wanted him more than she'd admitted. To hide that fact, and her confusion-over the depth of the wanting, she pulled him close, burying her face in the crook of his neck, inhaling him in, thinking he smelled so delicious she could gobble him up in one bite.

"You're killing me here." He took a deep breath as well, as if he wanted to take in her very essence, then nibbled at her throat, nudging his way beneath the strap of her tank to kiss her collarbone before he bit her shoulder. "Killing me."

The fire was at her back, snapping away with strength now and giving off a delicious heat. Or maybe that was him. He tossed aside her beanie, unraveled her braid and sank his fingers into her beanie-head hair, bringing her face back up for another soul-searching kiss, until all she could think about was his touch and how it made her feel. His fingers danced over her throat, down between her breasts to just over her pounding heart. "You're wearing too many clothes, too." He traced the edging of her tank over the curve of first one breast and then the other. Beneath the thin material, her nipples had long ago beaded into two tight, aching buds.

"Mmm." He cupped the small weight of both, his thumbs rubbing the tips while he kissed her slowly and deeply. Half gone, she went for the zipper on his jeans, the rasp of the metal echoing in her ears while he slipped her tank down. Beneath, she was naked, and a low, appreciative moan escaped him at the sight of her.

She slid her fingers into his opened jeans while he eyed the distance to the couch. He peeled the tank and the denim down her legs together, moaned at how wet her panties were, then tossed those aside, too.

And tumbled her to the fluffy couch.

With a breathless laugh she lifted her head to look at him. At the look on his face, the laugh backed up in her throat. No matter what she told herself, or him, this wasn't going to be just quick and fun and light, but something more, something deeper. In quick denial of that, she kissed him so hard that she once again lost herself in the way he touched her, lost herself in the sexy growl he made low in his throat when she reached inside his jeans and wrapped her fingers around his hot, silky, thick length.

With her help, he kicked off the rest of his clothes and then came down over her again, braced on his forearms, cradling her face in his hands, the plump cushions of the couch swallowing them both up. Between her legs he was hard and heavy, and she lifted her hips, needing him inside like she needed her next breath. But he held back.

"Lily." His thumbs glided along her jaw, up and back, a hypnotic touch that made her gaze a prisoner of his. Then he replaced his thumbs with his mouth, a light teasing touch that had her trying to turn her head to catch it with hers, wanting the oblivion of another soul-shattering kiss, but he evaded her, damn it, dipping down to taste her throat, and then farther down to a breast, which he drew into his mouth, pulling a cry out of her that she couldn't hold in.

With his tongue, his hands, his teeth, he drove her up, until unbelievably, she was quivering on the very edge of an orgasm. She'd never come with just a few hot kisses and a mouth on her breast before, but she could now, oh God, she almost could if he'd just touch— She wiggled a bit, shaky and desperate, trying to rub herself against him, but again he pulled back just enough. With a growl of frustration, she spread her legs farther, and he settled more deeply between them, rocking, the rhythm of it making her cry out again. *Yes!* But still unable to get to the big bang fast enough, she reared up and fastened her mouth to his, reaching between them to guide him home.

"Wait." He dropped his forehead to hers and gulped in air. "I want to—"

"This. I want *this*." She arched up, and with a rough groan, he sank into her.

Fierce and intense pleasure rippled through her, but it still wasn't enough. She writhed beneath him, panting, trembling, *desperate*. She couldn't remember how long it had been since she'd felt a man's weight on her like this, but clearly it'd been too long, a fact proven when he pulled out and she nearly sobbed.

"Condom," he said thickly, and dipped his head, taking a breast into his mouth again, suckling gently, then harder, yet again building the heat and tension and need to unbearable heights.

Then he lifted his head, his eyes on fire, and she thought, *Oh now. Now*. But he only ran a hand over her calf, her knee, the inside of her thigh. He brushed a finger over her, and she nearly jerked off the couch. With a heated smile, he did it again, stroking the pad of his finger up and down, then up again, dipping into her wet heat, spreading it, intently watching his every movement as he came back to her very center every time, circling it, over and over.

Her breath came in short pants, all of which backed up in her throat when he lowered his head and replaced his fingers with his tongue. Her groan mixed with his now, and she began to skitter out of control. The shudders began deep inside her, bursting when he pressed her thighs open even farther and suckled her deep into his mouth.

And this wasn't the little pop she was used to, either, no quick satisfaction of a basic need, but an implosion of heat and lights and sensory overload, made all the more overwhelming and confusing because she felt her emotions tangle up in it.

He let her down carefully, sweetly, and feeling battered, she came back to herself. His eyes smiled. "Hi," he said.

"Hi, yourself. *More.*"

"Hold that thought." He reached onto the floor for his jeans and pulled a condom out from the pocket. He ripped the packet open with his teeth, then rolled it on himself—yet another surprisingly erotic sensation, watching his fingers handle that basic necessity.

"I wanted to take this slow," he said. "I wanted to last all night, but watching you fall apart did me in." He kissed her, hard and fierce, using his tongue in a way that left her weak. Need slammed back into her, closing hot and greedy around her, and she moaned, surging up to drape herself around him. She rolled, intending to swap positions so she could straddle him and take matters into her own hands, but they fell off the couch to the floor.

She found herself pinned beneath him and, laughing breathlessly, wrapped her legs around his waist. "Logan. Now."

"Yeah, now." Digging his fingers into her hips, he drove himself into her with an erection that filled her to bursting.

She closed her eyes. She always closed her eyes, lost in the sensation of wet flesh dragging on wet flesh, but he slid his fingers into her hair. "Lily. Look at me."

And so she did, locked her eyes on his hot, fierce ones. "Keep looking at me," he whispered, and began to move.

She could do little else now, held captive by his dark, opaque gaze, by his hard body thrusting into hers. She felt it build again, even bigger this time, and then…she burst.

"Oh, yeah, that's the way," he said, his voice rough and gravelly. He sank his fingers into her hair, holding her head cradled in his palms as she cried out and trembled, and then he followed her over.

8

WHEN LILY COULD BREATHE again, she opened her eyes. She lay flat on her back on the floor of her living room, sprawled naked and damp and stuck to another body. A most excellent body that even now could affect her heart rate.

Logan pressed a kiss to her throat and turned her head toward his. Propping his head on his hand, he sent her a sexy smile.

Helplessly, she returned it.

He stroked his free hand down her torso, letting it come to rest just beneath her breast. His thumb lazily swiped at her nipple, which responded immediately to his touch. "Mmm." Bending over her, he sucked it into his mouth.

She heard her low, soft moan and pulled back, surprised that she could still want him. "Want something to eat?"

"No, thanks."

"I do."

He was silent while she got to her feet, hunting up the clothing they'd haphazardly tossed around them.

Where the hell was her tank top?

"Lily? You okay?"

"Are you kidding?" She let out a laugh meant to convince them both that she was totally okay, *more* than. She was merely starving, not desperately trying to avoid looking into his amazing eyes, hiding from the truth.

She was scared. Bone-deep scared that what they'd just done didn't seem like the usual wham, bam, thank you, ma'am. Worse, she had a feeling that she could have him every night of the three he had left here and she'd still feel the same way.

She couldn't find her panties so she shimmied into her jeans without them, and then tugged on Logan's T-shirt, which was inside out. With a growl of frustration, she ripped it off, and then found it tugged out of her hands.

Logan had gotten to his feet. Apparently not feeling the same need to dress, he stood before her gloriously naked and turned his T-shirt right side out for her, then let it drift down over her head. His fingers straightened the sleeves, and then he looked into her eyes. "What's the matter?"

"I told you, I'm hungry." She turned away but he snagged her and turned her back.

"What's the matter?" he repeated softly, making her throat tight and her eyes burn, which really bit. She never cried, and certainly not over a guy. She wasn't going to start now.

He stroked a strand of her undoubtedly wild hair off her face with a warm, callused finger. "Want me to guess?"

"I'm just—"

"Hungry. I know. What happened, Lily, did I get too close there for a moment?"

"Don't be ridiculous." She backed away and his hands fell from her. "Popcorn or toast? I don't have much of a selection because I usually head down to the cafeteria when I need something."

He looked at her for a long beat. "It doesn't matter."

"Popcorn," she decided and whirled away from his amazing body, from the look in his eyes that said he wanted to gobble her up whole again, as soon as he inhaled her thoughts.

Thoughts that weren't up for public consumption.

She stuck the popcorn into the microwave and watched the light come on, concentrated on the bag growing larger and larger, and when the microwave beeped, she nearly jumped. She took the bag out, carefully opened it and started munching.

Then and only then did she turn. Logan had pulled on his jeans but hadn't fastened them. He sat on her couch, legs out, arms spread over the backs of the cushions, watching her.

"It's hot," she said inanely, and stuffed another handful into her mouth.

"Come here."

"Yeah. Okay." She sat down next to him, leaving a wide space between them for her mental health, but he turned to face her, surrounding her with his bare chest and long arms, and it wasn't an unpleasant surrounding sort of thing at all. Neither were the odd little throbbing pulses her body kept giving off. The aftermath of hot, panting sex, she supposed.

His fingers stroked her shoulder, the back of her

neck, and when she sighed, eventually sagging back, he pulled her in even closer. "So what do you do when you're not working?" he asked, reaching for some popcorn.

She opened her mouth and then closed it. She laughed.

"What?" he asked, drawing his finger over the skin on her shoulders.

"You want to talk and cuddle."

"Sure."

She stared at him but he wasn't kidding. He was a man, a red-blooded, earthy, sexual, *gorgeous* man. And they'd already had sex. So why the hell wasn't he running? Instead, he simply stretched out a little more, those long, long legs taking up a good amount of space, his broad chest looking scrumptious by firelight as he waited for her to answer him.

"I'm nearly always working," she said.

"I can see that. How about when the season is over?"

"We open the trails up for hiking and mountain biking."

He winced. "You must rescue people all year long."

"Yeah, but I didn't always work like this. Just this last year since my grandma died and I became manager. I used to be ski-patrol director, and in the other seasons I was activity director."

"You can't keep up this pace, Lily. You're trying to do it all."

She smiled sadly. "Well, it'd be easier to give up the outdoor stuff if I was loving the management side of things."

"Do you ever get away from here?"

"Once in a while I manage to see friends in town. Sometimes we travel around, checking out the other resorts. How about you? What do you do with yourself when you're not working?"

"I haven't been on vacation in years." His fingers continued to play at the back of her neck, making her want to stretch and purr like a kitten. "In fact, it's been a long time since I've been as relaxed as I am right now. Years."

"You haven't had sex in years?"

"I haven't been on *vacation* in years." He had laugh lines fanning out from his eyes, and they crinkled now. "Although to tell you the truth, I haven't had sex like we just did in a very long time."

"Me, either," she admitted softly, his ensuing smile making her feel as if she were the only woman on the planet. "So why haven't you vacationed in so long?"

He lifted a shoulder. "I love what I do and just rarely feel the need to get away from it."

Right. Yet another example of why this heart-palpitating urge to grab him and never let go was so very bad. He loved his life, his job, his everything. Hundreds and hundreds of miles away.

"My brothers would appreciate this place," he said, still playing with her skin.

"They both ski?"

"When they get a chance. Right now Tom is out on a ship in the mid-Atlantic somewhere, helping to keep the waters safe from terrorists and drug dealers. Paul is in the Gulf, doing the same thing."

His voice was filled with pride, something she knew was missing in her own siblings' voices when they discussed her. "How often do you see each other?"

"If you'd asked me when I was still at home, I'd have said too damn much. My dad worked long hours and I had to be mom, dad, brother, enforcer." He grinned. "I'm glad those days are over."

She ran her gaze over his fond smile and something within her softened. It was her guard, she discovered. She was losing it. "You're a man who's used to being needed. A man used to the weight of responsibility. So how come you're not married? Or in a relationship?"

"My work isn't really conducive to that. The hours alone would drain a relationship dry. And though most women claim they're attracted to a man with a dangerous profession, the reality is they're not. It's a lot to ask of someone, and I just haven't asked."

So he saw love as an obligation, something no one understood more than she. Love *was* an obligation, and it was also a pain in her ass.

"So what holds *you* back from being involved?" he asked. "Your own fierce independence? Or the wall you put up when someone gets too close?"

"Nothing holds me back from anything."

"That's right. You're fearless." His fingers were stroking her, lulling her, and she realized she'd settled back into the crook of his shoulder, against his side, as if she belonged there. Her hand had fallen low on his flat belly, rather shockingly possessively, as if she had the right. She stared at her hand on that vulnerable spot beneath his belly button, so flat and sinewy and male, and wriggled her fingers, thinking that it was his own fault her mind was wandering back to sex. He should have gone running when he had the chance. Instead, he'd stayed to talk, to cuddle, and he'd have to face the consequences…. She slid her fingers down.

"Mmm," rumbled from deep in his chest. With the denim already unfastened, leaving his waistband loose, she reached the pot of gold with no trouble at all, laughing softly, triumphantly, when he turned out to be already hard. "Again, Lily?"

"Oh, yes." She stood only to strip her jeans back off before she fell on top of him. "Again."

LOGAN WOKE UP TO AN affectionate tap on his bare ass. He was sprawled facedown and sideways across Lily's bed, with all the bedding wadded on the floor. Lifting his head, he squinted into her light brown eyes.

Vague images of her beneath him, over him, panting, by turns demanding and whimpering, turned into vivid memories, and he grinned.

"Oh, no, ace." Fully dressed, she backed up. "We're done."

Normally he'd be chomping at the bit now that he was awake, needing to get to work, but he didn't feel like chomping at anything but Lily's gorgeous, curvy bod. "Come here."

"I've gotta run."

Hmm. Seemed Lily was doing all the chomping at the bit for the both of them. He pushed himself up, but she put a hand on his shoulder.

"Don't get up, I just wanted to say goodbye." She blushed, which intrigued him given all they'd done to and for each other in the long hours of the night. "I didn't want to just leave you a note."

"I appreciate that."

She stood there in her loose black cargo ski pants and a snug red turtleneck, looking like winter personified. He sat up on the edge of the bed and pulled her between his spread legs, wrapping his arms around her middle, putting his head on her chest and hugging her.

For a moment her hands fluttered at his shoulders, then she slid them around him and squeezed. "Last night was…"

Tilting his head up, he smiled at her. "Was…?"

"Nice."

He laughed, watching her mouth curve—the same mouth that had been crying his name in a desperate mantra only a little while ago. "Nice? Last night was *nice?*"

"Okay, it was pretty damn amazing," she consented. "And wild fun to boot, which is always a pleasant surprise. But I'm not sure it's something we should repeat."

"Why not?"

Something flashed in her eyes. Unease? *Fear?*

What the hell was that about?

And then he got it.

She was afraid she couldn't keep it to just fun, not with him.

"Look, this was supposed to be a good time for what's left of your vacation," she said cautiously. "Even a *great* time. But that's all I've got to give."

"How do you know a good time isn't all I have to give, as well?"

"Is it?"

He watched her hold her breath, looking ready to bolt if he so much as said boo.

Or admitted that hell, no, it wasn't enough. "Yes."

"Promise?" she whispered.

"Do you ask that of everyone you sleep with?"

She let out a disparaging sigh.

"Do you?"

"No."

He found that fascinating. Hell, *she* was fascinating. He slid his hands down her pretty damn amazing body, cupping her sweet ass, nuzzling his face between her breasts. "I'll see you later."

"Promise me, Logan."

He bit the inner curve of her right breast, smiling when she shivered. "I promise to see you later."

"*Logan.*"

He sighed. "Fine. I promise you're a good time, and nothing but a good time."

"Okay." She backed up. "Okay, then." Beneath her tight red turtleneck, her nipples were two taut points, begging for his attention. Her eyes revealed the arousal, and also a huge relief.

He felt the arousal, too, but not the relief. "Let me walk you out."

"No, that's all right."

He frowned when she turned away and moved to the door, shutting it behind her without a backward look. "Wow," he said to no one. Flopping to his back on her mattress, he studied the ceiling. Hard to believe it, but she wasn't being coy or playing with him. She'd said what she meant and meant what she'd said.

Fun, wild sex only. Nothing more.

Any red-blooded male would be dancing. He was dancing.

And if a small part of him wished things were different, he could keep that to himself. After all, he was only here for a few more days. Then it'd be back to his world.

Sans Lily.

9

LILY GLANCED AT HER WATCH—7:30 a.m.—and tried not to imagine what she could be doing right this minute if an hour ago she hadn't looked into Logan's eyes and panicked.

God, it had felt good lying in bed with him wrapped around her like a pretzel, all sleek skin and hard sinew and easy sexiness. But she'd gotten up. Leaped up and out the door was more like it, mostly because she *hadn't* wanted to. She was going to have enough trouble not getting too attached for the next three nights, she didn't need to lounge around and relive the mind-blowing night.

And it had been mind-blowing, she'd give him that. She'd always equated sex with the subtle quenching of a thirst. A nice little treat, a release of the need, the end. At least until the next time she got thirsty.

Nothing about last night had been a nice little treat, an easy release of need. In fact, she felt more needy now than she had before, even though they'd hardly slept, unable to keep their hands—or mouths—off each other. Just thinking about it made her body hum.

What she needed now was to clear her head, and there was only one way to do that. On the slopes. She'd spent a few moments at her desk. She'd checked on the cafeteria. Everything seemed to be running smoothly. The bar was dark, and so was the shop, which wouldn't open for another hour. No one would be in their offices yet, and with no emergencies lurking, she went to her ski locker. She'd catch a ride up on a snowcat with her patrollers, who'd be out checking on the mountain and the conditions.

Then she'd take a run, get some very cold air burning through her lungs, and she would not, would absolutely *not*, daydream or fantasize about one incredibly sexy Logan White.

"Going to take in a few runs?"

She jerked in surprise and found the incredibly sexy Logan White standing there in the flesh. His hair was wet, as if he'd rushed out of the shower, and if she wasn't mistaken, he smelled like her mangomelon shampoo and matching soap. He wore his ski pants, but in concession to what looked to be a warmer, sunnier day than yesterday, wore a SAR T-shirt layered over a long sleeved T-shirt, no jacket.

When she just stared at him, he smiled a bit grimly and stepped closer, lifting a finger to her chin, which alerted her to the fact her mouth had fallen open.

Then he kissed her right on that mouth. "I thought about you in your shower. When I went back to my room for fresh clothes. When I breathe. How about some company?"

She opened her eyes and cleared her throat. It'd been just a little kiss, insignificant when compared to what they'd already shared, and yet it jump-started her heart the way the steepest hill on the mountain would have. Or maybe it was the fact that he'd searched her out. "Okay."

He cocked his head. "You look surprised. You didn't think I'd want to spend some time with you?"

"You just spent some time with me." *Naked. In bed. Driving me out of my mind with your fingers, your tongue, your teeth—* She had to lock her wobbly knees and ignore the heat building between her thighs. "I guess I thought you'd be done."

He just looked at her for a long moment. "Maybe I'm different, Lily."

"Are you?"

"Does that scare you?"

"I've told you. Nothing scares me."

"You're such a liar." He cupped his palm around the nape of her neck, nudged her into him so that he could kiss her again. His mouth was warm, familiar now, and this time when he lifted his head, her body was throbbing, her thoughts were spinning, her world, completely off its axis and…and he laughed.

"You're looking at me like maybe you'd rather go back to bed than ski," he murmured, just a little too sure of himself.

"Don't flatter yourself, ace. I'd rather ski any day."

"Are you sure about that?"

Hell, no. "Very." She grabbed her skis this time and slammed her locker, walking out, not looking back to see if he followed.

Her nipples were hard, damn him, and between her thighs, she was damp, proving her one big, fancy liar.

THEY HITCHED A RIDE UP THE mountain with her grooming crew on a large snowcat, then made their way to the east-facing slopes, chasing the early sun down long, long trails that ran the gamut of terrain, some narrow with lots of trees, some wide and clear. For two hours Logan skied and watched Lily do the same, exhilaration flowing through his veins.

When she finally stopped, shaking herself free of some loose snowy powder, she laughed. Her eyes were lit, her cheeks were rosy, and as she glanced over at him, her hair whipping out of her helmet, her smile stretching from ear to ear, his heart tipped on its side. "You look pretty satisfied."

"Being out here like this should be a requirement for relieving stress."

So should what they'd shared last night. His own stress relief was usually done in a gym with a punching bag, or on the streets with his running shoes.

But skiing his brains out worked, too.

"The wind's kicked up," she said and got on her walkie-talkie. She consulted with base, then clipped it back on her belt. "We'll have to watch the upper lifts, might have to close them."

Either way, she'd have her hands full soon enough. Her day would get crazy, as he suspected it always did. But for now she stood there on top of her mountain, her world, stripping out of her fleece, tying it around her waist, leaving just the snug red turtleneck. Bending over, she ran her gloved hands down the top of her legs. "My thighs are burning."

He had burning parts, too, but not his thighs. Between them. "Come here."

Her eyes locked with his and she licked her lips, a telling little gesture he'd noticed she used when nervous. "Every time you say that, you end up kissing me stupid. I lost a lot of brain cells last night, and can't really afford to lose any more—"

He simply hooked an elbow around her neck and tugged her close, swallowing her words with his mouth.

A soft murmur of acquiescence escaped her and she slid her fingers into his hair, holding him to her.

As if he intended to let go. Nope, no way. "Tonight," he whispered, nipping his way along her throat beneath her helmet strap. "I want to see you tonight."

She opened her eyes and searched his while all around them the wind whipped up, harder and faster. "Do you?"

"Oh, yeah. And for every night I have left." He ran his thumb over her full lower lip. "If you end up working late again, you know where my room is. Don't be shy."

She dragged her teeth over that lower lip now, torturing it in a way he wanted to do himself. Her hair, hanging out from below her helmet, blew across her face. He stroked it away, then leaned in and kissed her again, deeper this time. She opened to him, and the heat and voracious need for her slammed right back, as if they'd not assuaged that need all night long. He had no idea how he could want her this way, again, still, but it was there shimmering between them, through them—

Her walkie-talkie chirped, and Lily jumped back as if she'd been jolted by a live wire. She stared at him, eyes unreadable, mouth still wet as she lifted the radio and checked in.

She looked like a woman good and shocked over what should have been a damn simple kiss. He knew the feeling, because nothing had been simple about any of this, not since the moment he'd first laid eyes on her.

"I have to go," she said, making him realize she'd put her radio back on her belt.

"The lifts are going to close already."

"The upper ones, yes, after only letting a few people on. But that's not it."

"You have a rescue."

"There's a crew there already, but they can't get a helicopter out in this wind so he has to be skied down. And…they sorta need me there."

"Want some help?"

She looked at him for one heartbeat. Two. "Yes," she finally said. "Sure."

They traversed the mountain in the increasingly fierce wind, heading over to the west side. Their mood was different now, somber instead of joyful. When the steep, craggy cliffs jutted out over the basin far below, appearing to fall off into thin air, she stopped. A risky-looking rescue was already well under way, with some patrollers gathered around, and he wondered why Lily had been called over.

"Here."

Logan looked at the craziest-looking cliff he'd ever seen on a slope and let out a slow whistle.

"There is a very fine line between hobby and mental illness."

Beside him, Lily choked out a laughing agreement. "Apparently he hit a rock and slid off to the side. One patroller has already rappelled down. The victim is wedged, and has what looks like two broken arms." She shook her head and a spasm crossed her face. Worry.

She was worried about whoever had been stupid enough to go over, but Logan was thinking the victim was lucky if that's all he'd broken. "You have two out-of-bounds markers up. Why would someone go down there?"

"There's always the daredevils who see the markers as nothing more than a challenge, no matter what we do. The thing is, the locals know exactly how far to fling themselves out right there so they don't get killed on the rocks. They're supposed to land on the outcropping below them."

"It's seriously insane."

She didn't say anything.

"You've done it," he guessed, watching her face.

She lifted a shoulder. "When I was much more stupid than I am now. There've been a couple of boarder movies made from right here. You might have seen some of the footage."

"Where they fall an unbelievable distance and then either land on their feet or tumble down the mountain in a heap of equipment and limbs?"

She smiled grimly. "I was lucky enough to land my attempt."

He marveled at her. Not just at the daredevil,

come-what-may persona—which was utterly genuine, not forced or faked as it might have been—but at the fact that she had such intelligence, such heart to go with all that toughness. "What's taking them so long to get him up?"

"There's an unexpected complication." She sighed, clicked out of her skis and moved into the fray.

In spite of the vicious wind, they'd brought out the ropes and had created a Z-rig, a zigzagging combination of rope and manpower. Because they stood on an expert run, where the lifts were now closed, there weren't any spectators around, which Logan knew would make the job easier.

This close to the edge, the dizzying height rushed up to meet him, a sensation increased by the bruising winds. He thought of anyone purposely skiing off here, of Lily doing it, and had to admit that she had more guts than he did.

He watched her get into gear, feeling far more tense than whenever *he* geared up for a rescue. Then she was going over the edge, and he held his breath.

"Why is she going down?" Logan asked Chris over a gust of wind that made him stagger back. The two front men on the Z-rig swore and scrambled to tighten their hold on Lily, and Logan nearly crunched his teeth to dust.

"It was a request," Chris said.

"What do you mean, a request?"

"The victim asked for her specifically."

Logan stared at him for a moment, then down at Lily. The wind kicked up again, gusting hard, blowing up a cloud of powder, and suddenly everything went white. Lily vanished. Hell, everything vanished for the longest moment of Logan's life, as he was forced to wait for the snow to settle again. When it finally did, both Logan and Chris leaped to the edge.

Lily was still there.

Logan was well familiar with emergencies such as this: bad weather, worse conditions for the climb and an injured vic. Always, he calmly handled it, all of it.

But he found he couldn't handle this, not with Lily dangling fifty feet in the chasm and the wind beating at her as if she was nothing more than a rag doll.

The brutal wind didn't let up, and on the next harsh gust, the light snow once again went airborne, brushing free of the rocks, completely choking off their vision and creating another full-blown white-out situation.

It was the eeriest thing. Logan could have put both hands right in front of his face and he wouldn't have seen them, so he stood there and clenched them into fists, swearing helplessly while the seconds passed, long, heart-pounding seconds, because while they were blinded, no one could keep track of the victim.

Or Lily.

Logan was known for his patience, but every ounce of it had deserted him, replaced by a bone-gnawing desperation that he should have been used to after the hundreds of rescues in his past. But it never got easier, and that it was someone he knew in trouble— something too close to when, just a few months ago, he'd been forced to leave Wyatt and Leah on a houseboat in the middle of a twister—made it all the more chilling. He didn't care to ever repeat this fear.

What seemed like eons passed, but it was probably only thirty seconds before the gust finally died and the snow settled. Lily was still down there, on the rope, against the rock. Not moving.

Logan and Chris pressed as close to the edge as they dared and shouted her name.

She tilted her head up, brushed the snow from her goggles and lifted a hand.

"She's okay," Chris said in clear relief.

Insides quivering, Logan nearly sank to his knees. Everyone around them breathed the same relief, and with tension taut enough to be cut with a knife, they went back to the rescue efforts.

Logan moved to the Z-rig, adding his hands to the fray without hesitation, wishing like hell he could be the one down on the rope. Twice more the winds kicked up, and twice more everything stopped. With Lily dangling off a rope over a cliff.

On the last time, the wind whistled and raged around them for an agonizing three full minutes, and this time when they could see, Lily wasn't so quick to wave.

Logan held his breath, and next to him so did Chris. "Come on, come on," Chris muttered, fingering his walkie-talkie, hesitating to use it. Logan knew why: Chris didn't want Lily having to reach for it, occupying a hand she needed. "She'll call if she needs something," he said.

But would she? Logan knew her now, or was beginning to. The woman was stubborn and unbelievably tough. He thought maybe she was tougher than some of the guys he'd worked with for years, and with that came a sense of personal indestructibility. He knew this firsthand because he'd felt it himself. Something about being on a rescue, with lives in the balance and the elements battering everything, changed a person's perspective, made them feel immortal somehow. All that mattered in that moment was getting the victim to safety.

Lily felt the same way now, he just knew it. Which made his fear for her escalate. It wasn't often he felt helpless, but he felt the greasy weight of it now. He'd rarely been on this side of a rescue before, and he didn't like it.

He watched grimly as she finally landed on the rock far below and bent over the victim with the other patroller.

Chris brought out his walkie-talkie. "How is he?"

"Pissed," came Lily's voice. "And amused that you guys got me down here."

"He demanded it," Chris said in exasperation. "Said he was going to wait there until either you came or spring arrived."

"Well now he can listen to me bitch at his stupidity. Send down the litter."

"Who are we talking about?" Logan demanded as the crew sent down a flat litter for Lily and the other patroller to get the victim into so that he could be hauled back up the cliff. Whoever the jerk was, Logan felt the urge to wrap his fingers around his neck and squeeze—

"Pete Wheeler. You might have heard of him, he's won gold in boarding the past two X Games. You know, the extreme adventure games."

"He's local?"

"Yeah. He's also…" He shut his mouth.

"What? An idiot?"

"Lily's on-again, off-again boyfriend."

Well, hell, he'd asked, hadn't he? And anyway, it didn't matter. He was only here for another few days. What had he really thought, that they'd actually make some kind of go of this? Of course not, she'd told him right up front that this was just fun.

She'd made him promise the same.

Just fun. Yeah, this was a riot a minute.

When Pete's litter came over the top, Chris and two others grabbed him, preparing to ski him down to meet the ambulance waiting for him at the lodge. Lily came up next and dropped to the snow in exhaustion. Logan was right there. It was all he could do not to haul her close, but instead, he examined the nasty scratch along her chin and jaw. "You got slammed into the rocks."

"Saw stars," she agreed grimly and backed from his hands to move to Pete. She looked down at him, and he looked right back at her, pale and wanly smiling.

"Knew you'd come get me," he said, making her laugh softly.

"You're such a fool." She touched his cheek with a tenderness that shouldn't have surprised Logan. Hell, she'd touched him like that, too.

"A fool who wanted to keep up with you," Pete said.

"I haven't skied off that cliff in years."

"Ah." He closed his eyes. "Aunt Debbie's been pulling my leg, regaling me with stories of your craziness."

"*Old* craziness," Lily corrected, and sighed. "No one ever gets that. Enjoy your ride, Pete."

"*You* take me down."

"Oh, no." She stroked the hair back from his forehead. "I got you off the mountain. Now take your medicine like a big boy."

"Yeah." Pete let out a careful breath, grimacing at the pain. "I didn't mean for you to get hurt, Lil." He jerked his chin in the direction of the wrist she held against her belly. "I'll save you the bed next to mine at the hospital."

"Don't hold your breath." She nodded to Chris, who with a partner began to ski Pete down the hill.

"You need some medical attention," Logan said to her.

"It's just a scratch."

He gestured to her wrist.

"Oh, this?" She opened and closed her fingers. "Not broken."

"Why didn't you say something after you'd been hit? Any of us would have hauled you up and taken your place."

"I was fine."

"You're always fine."

"That's right," she said cautiously, her smile fading. "What's the matter?"

"You risked yourself needlessly."

"Needlessly? There was an injured party down there and I went after him. That's a part of the life out here. And I'd have thought you, of all people, got that."

That she was right didn't ease his tension or make him feel any better. She'd turned away from him now, gathering a rope to entwine it. He snatched it from her and did the job himself. "Go get some ice," he said, probably more roughly than he'd intended. But screw it. He'd let her mess with his head, and that was so far from his usual realm of not caring enough, it shook him to the very core.

She stared at him for a long moment, then backed away. "All right. Thank you."

And then she was gone.

10

WHEN SHE GOT DOWN THE MOUNTAIN, Lily cleaned up her cuts, wrapped her wrist to match her knee and dug into work. There were other fires that had to be put out all over the resort, such as someone posting a party notice for that night in the bar on the bulletin board in her name. Obviously a joke, but she removed it—thankfully before Sara or Gwyneth caught wind of it.

Or maybe not a joke. Maybe the same person who'd messed with her food delivery.

Aunt Debbie happened by as Lily was tossing the party flyer in the trash, and lifted a brow at her. "Mom always wondered if you'd outgrow your party years."

"She knew I had," Lily said.

"I guess that's why you inherited." Debbie's smile went from playful to wistful. "One of us had to grow up and be responsible, huh? Oh well, it wasn't ever going to be me, that's for sure." Surprising Lily, she pulled her in for a hug. "Thanks for putting up with me."

Since Lily sensed a lingering sadness alongside the usual mocking humor, she endured the embrace.

"I'm sorry you're sad." She wished for Sara, who was better at this nurturing, mothering thing.

"Are you?" Aunt Debbie pulled back and laughed. "Well, that's unexpectedly sweet. You must be mellowing with old age."

"Am not."

"Used to be no one was badder than you. You never took anyone's crap."

"I don't take any now, either. Speaking of which, stop telling stories about me."

"But you're a legend."

"Pete took a crazy chance today because of your stories."

"Pete's a big boy, he should have known better. See?" She clucked Lily under the chin. "You're not yelling at me. Definitely mellowing. And you know what else, kid? I'm not the only sad one here."

Lily thought about that as she went back to work. Was she mellowing? Sad? All she knew was that the day-to-day running of this place was eating away at the joy and peace the mountain gave her, and she was tired, so damn tired, from trying to keep up with everything.

Maybe that's what Aunt Debbie had seen—pure exhaustion.

She thought about that while she sorted her way through the piles on her desk as evening came. Gwyneth showed up and reported that the cafeteria looked filled to brimming and that Logan had joined a group of dispatchers and cops from L.A. who'd come up to ski. Sounded like so much fun that Lily rushed through the expense report she was working on, but by the time she got to the bar, she was too late.

"They took the moonlit trails on rented snowmobiles," Matt told her, drying glasses and watching her carefully. "I suggested it."

"Oh. That's...nice." She sat on a bar stool and joined him in drying.

"Didn't know you were going to go back for seconds."

Her gaze whipped to his.

"It's not like you."

"I've gone out with guys more than once."

"Name one."

"Pete."

"Yes, but he's a ski bum who shows up on this mountain once, maybe twice, a year. You've always been safe pretending to date him."

Lily shook her head. "Matt?"

"Yeah?"

"Shut up."

He grinned. "Not until you take back calling me a sap."

"You are a sap. A sap who has to build me new shelves."

He grumbled at that and moved away to serve a customer.

Lily's job of irritating him now complete, she got into her car and drove to town to visit Pete at the hospital.

He was flat on his back, casted up and suitably high on pain meds. He grinned like a lunatic at the sight of her.

She couldn't help but sigh at the bigger-than-life athlete, tall, angular and so Swede with his blond, blue-eyed good looks, lying still and broken. "You're such a lucky bastard."

"How's that?"

"You could be dead. God, that was stupid today."

"Hey, you're supposed to be nice to me." He tried to shift and winced. Leaning in, Lily helped him get a pillow behind him for comfort, making him sigh. "You know why I never asked you to marry me, right?" he asked.

She pulled his blankets smooth and patted his arm. "Because being attached to one woman gives you hives?"

"Well, there's that." He sighed. "I watched you come down that mountain today. You put your life on the line for me, and I realized something."

"That you're a selfish SOB?"

His smile was weak. "That, too. You're a great catch, Lily. I should have—"

She put her fingers gently over his lips. "Don't." Even though they went back a couple of years, they'd never been a real couple, partly due to his women addiction, partly due to her own commitment issues. In fact, they hadn't been together at all for some time, and looking at him now, she felt a softness, a genuine affection, but not the heat. Not a single spark. "I came to tell you that I'm sorry you were hurt. Get better, Pete, soon. But when you do, stay off my cliffs."

He stared at her for a long moment. "You're really over me, aren't you?"

"Quite."

He smiled as his eyes closed. "You'll change your mind. You have before."

"No, I won't."

His smile dissolved and he opened his eyes. "It's that skier you were with today, isn't it?"

She scrambled for the denial, just a little too quickly. "I've only known him a few days."

"Days, years, minutes. Doesn't matter when it's the real thing."

"Like you would know the real thing if it bit you on the ass."

He laughed, then grimaced in pain. "Yeah. But you're the real thing, Lily. I'm just an idiot. Be happy, babe."

"You, too."

"I will, soon as you get out of here so I can get the pretty nurse on duty to come make me feel better."

Lily laughed, kissed him goodbye, then drove back to the resort, feeling each and every ache and bruise. She went to her apartment and took a hot, hot shower, thinking sleep would cure her. Then she proceeded to stare at the ceiling while the clocked ticked off the minutes. Then the hour.

She didn't want sleep. She wanted...

Logan.

Days, years, minutes. Doesn't matter when it's the real thing. Pete's words echoed in her head as she dressed again and made her way through the quiet lodge.

The real thing.

She'd told Pete he wouldn't recognize it if it reared up and bit him, and she'd always assumed the same thing about herself. She didn't want to recognize it because the real thing didn't fit into her life.

Love, if it existed, was a pain in the ass. It obligated. It forced a responsibility for someone else's feelings. It disappointed.

But lust…now lust was right up her alley.

She found herself in front of Logan's room.

Yeah, lust worked.

She hadn't seen him since Pete's hair-raising, ulcer-inducing rescue, and given how he'd looked at her after, as if he wanted to both shake her and kiss her and not in any particular order, that was probably a good thing. She'd needed her cool up there today, had needed to be in calm control despite how scared she'd been. She didn't know if she was feeling slightly smothered by his intense reaction or just overwhelmed by the strong emotion implied by it.

She lifted her hand to knock, then lowered it again. What the hell was she doing? Already she could hardly separate the sex they'd had with how mushy he made her feel.

Run.

She thought that sounded like a fine idea, and got to the end of the hallway. She stopped. Swore. Then paced back and stared at his door. Drew a deep breath. She was here for great sex. Just great sex. Sounded good. Sounded great.

Too great. Again she turned away, but suddenly the door opened and Logan stood there, bare-chested, wearing low-riding sweatpants and nothing else. Behind him, the room was dark, the bed mussed as if he'd been tossing and turning. *Thinking of her?*

"Did I wake you?" she asked.

"No."

She smiled softly and wished he'd smile back.

Wished even more that he'd grab her and hold on, touching her, kissing her, until her day was nothing but a memory. "You said no matter how late, right?"

"You tuck Pete into bed?"

Her smile faded. "I went to the hospital, yes." She paused. "Do you think there's something going on between Pete and me?"

"It doesn't matter what I think."

She cocked her head and studied his beautiful body, hard and tough, his eyes, dark and unreadable. She spent most of her life not caring what people thought of her, but with him, she found she cared. "Actually, yes, it does matter what you think."

"Why? I'm just a guest."

"You're more than just a guest to me."

"But this is just fun. Isn't that right, Lily?"

Trapped in her own web. She went a little cold inside. "Look, if I'd had a prior commitment with someone else, I would never have agreed to whatever this is that we're doing for the next three days. You'd better tell me you know that."

He tunneled his fingers through his hair, his raised arms delineating all the corded sinew in his biceps and shoulders. And as if she was still on that mountain precipice, hanging with her life in the balance, everything within her quivered with awareness and anticipation. But she'd had enough excitement for the day, more than her poor body could take. Done with this, she turned away, determined that this time, her feet would take her back to bed. Her own.

"Lily."

Her feet stopped. Turned her.

"*Hell.*" He scrubbed his hands over his face. "Look, seeing you put yourself on the line today—"

"You do stuff like that all the time at home."

"I know. *I know.* It makes no sense. I'm sorry." He blew out a harsh breath and looked miserable. "When the wind kicked up and you slipped…" He closed his eyes. "For the first time in my life I understood what it was like to be on the other end, on the watching end, and it nearly killed me. Lily—"

He might have said more but she stepped back to him and put a finger over his lips. "Sorry enough to make it up to me?"

"Yeah. Let me show you." Keeping his eyes on hers, he pulled her over the threshold, then shut the door. The lock clicked in like a bullet.

LOGAN HAD MEANT TO RESIST her, he really had, but one look into those challenging eyes and it'd been over. They didn't even make it to the bed. Instead, he slid his arms around her and she came hard against him, holding his face so that she could rain kisses over it. Staggered by her show of need and his own clawing hunger for her, he pressed her up against the door, freeing up his hands to do what he pleased.

And what he pleased was to take them both to the same mindless place they'd gone last night. She wore a long, loose sweater over leggings. Wrestling the sweater off, he tossed it over his shoulder then dropped to his knees before her and tugged down her leggings.

She had on a peach camisole and a matching thong that made him groan as he leaned in to press his mouth to her.

"Logan—"

She choked that off with a gasp when he yanked down the thong and stroked her with his tongue. Her fingers fisted in his hair as he urged her legs farther apart. The sight of her spread and vulnerable to him, revealing how aroused she was, drove him mad. He sucked her into his mouth. Her head thunked back against the door, her hips undulating in time with his tongue until she shuddered and exploded with abandon.

He groped for the pants he had over a chair, and the condom in the pocket. Lily would have slid weakly to the floor if he hadn't surged upright and caught her in time. "Hold on to me." He gripped her hips, groaning when she wrapped her legs around his waist. "Hold on."

"I am. I will." Her fingers dug into his shoulders. "Now, now, now."

He couldn't catch his breath, helpless against this vicious need for her. He struggled to get his sweats down and the condom on, and then finally, finally, thrust into her, burying himself to the hilt.

There was no holding back after that, not with her gripping him like a tight, wet, loving fist, not when she began to spiral again, convulsing around him. He felt himself drowning in her, drowning without a lifeline, letting go more completely than he ever had, and not caring as he buried his face in her hair and exploded so hard his toes curled. He had to slap a hand against the door, his arm rigid and quivering as he fought to maintain balance enough to hold them upright.

Exhausted, Lily's body relaxed and her head fell to his shoulder. "Mmm..."

Yeah, *mmm*. Somehow he found the energy to dump her on his bed, where they held on to each other and slept like the living dead.

11

AT DAWN, LILY TIPTOED OUT of Logan's room and quietly shut the door, then leaned back against it.

She had to get to work.

Or so she told herself.

Much better than thinking she was actually using any sort of avoidance technique, which she abhorred.

Aw, hell, she was using an avoidance technique. She closed her eyes and saw Logan again, looking gorgeous and rumpled all sprawled naked across his bed. She'd spent a good five minutes looking her fill before sneaking out into the hall, where she'd hopefully get to her own room and change before anyone realized she was still wearing yesterday's clothes—

"You taking up room cleaning now?"

Lily's eyes flew open and met the gaze of the one person she'd have liked to avoid this morning.

Gwyneth.

"Hey." Lily ran her hand down her undoubtedly wild hair. "What are you doing up so early?"

"Well, I'm not tiptoeing out of a guest's room looking like I've been ravished all night long, that's for certain. I wanted to get a head start on the receivables, but a guest needed an extra blanket and I just happened to get the call. Did you even look in the mirror?"

Lily tugged at her sweater.

"I'm talking about the love bite on your neck."

"Back off." But she put a finger to the spot on her neck as she moved past her sister.

Gwyneth grabbed her hand. Lily whipped around, prepared for battle, but in her sister's gaze was a soft worry. "Lily—"

"Not here." Lily glanced at Logan's door. "Not here." She started walking to her room. Gwyneth followed. "I'm taking a shower," Lily warned. "Alone."

But when she came back out of her room fifteen minutes later, her sister was leaning against the wall waiting for her. "I heard what you did yesterday for Pete, how scary and dangerous the rescue was. We have people for that—you no longer have to dangle off cliffs for a living."

Lily began to walk toward their offices. "I happen to be good at it."

"You have different responsibilities now. Bigger ones. You should have let someone else go."

"Really?" She stopped in the still-dark common room. "One of our employees?"

"Hell, yes. They're trained and paid for it—it's not a crime if there's a rescue and you're not involved. But it's over and done, and you're safe, so I can let that go. There's something else."

She meant some*one* else, of course. *Logan.* His name floated in the air silently between them.

"You shouldn't be sleeping with a guest, Lily. You shouldn't be—"

"I don't have time for the 'shouldn't be' lecture." She began walking again.

"Is that what you think I'm doing? Giving you a lecture?"

"Don't do this. Don't do that. Don't, don't, don't..."

"It's never stopped you before. Look, I love you, you know I do, but—"

"But. Love always comes with a damn but." And she'd spent too many years chafing at the restraints, pretending not to care that she met exactly no one's expectations. "Maybe I'm tired of you not seeing me. I've grown up, Gwyneth. Years ago. Open your eyes and see it. I can handle this. I *am* handling this."

Gwyneth just shook her head, and Lily wanted to scream in frustration. If this was love, it weighed a ton. Was it any wonder she'd never even attempted to find such an emotion in her own relationships with men?

"There's a staff meeting today."

Lily drew a deep breath but it didn't help. "I know, I set it up." She entered the office wing, then stopped in surprise.

Sara and Matt sat on Carrie's desk, making out. It didn't look easy, what with the baby in the way and the desk full of paperwork, but Matt had his arms possessively and protectively around his wife and a big hand spread wide over her belly.

That gesture scraped at a spot in Lily's stomach. No matter how crazy Sara was, or how laid-back Matt was, they were so in love, transcending all the dissention and discord around them to become this...this *unit* in a way that was both alien to Lily and yet somehow so goddamn attractive it made her throat close up.

"Oh, for God's sake," Gwyneth said. "Get a room."

Matt lifted his mouth off Sara's and grinned. "We would, but that's how we got into trouble in the first place."

Sara put her hand on his jaw and smiled up at him as if he was her entire world.

Lily sighed. It was cute. Beautiful, even. But not the world she'd chosen for herself. "Why is everyone up so early?"

"I have a doctor's appointment this afternoon." Sara patted her belly. "I came in to get my stuff done."

"And I drove her in." Matt smiled into Sara's eyes.

"Oh, goody." This from Gwyneth. "No more kissing on the desks."

Lily rolled her eyes, but her mind was still on what Gwyneth had said about risking herself. She looked at Sara and Matt, so wildly in love, and wondered if she was this gone over someone, would she still want to go on the crazy rescues? And if the worst happened, and she died…would she go with no regrets?

She loved her life, and would have sworn she gave it her all, without holding back.

But she did hold back.

She held back where maybe she shouldn't—in matters of the heart—and for the first time, she asked herself what she was missing by doing so.

Gwyneth kicked Matt's feet off Carrie's desk, then nudged Lily past the lovebirds and into her office.

Lily went straight to her desk and the piles there, determined to sidetrack Gwyneth from the line of questioning they were headed for. *Logan.* "Do you want to go over the summer brochures? The pictures came back, they're not bad at all. Oh, and the ads for the statewide campaign are due today, and I haven't even had time to look at them…. Wait. Where are they?" She flipped through the piles, no longer trying for a distraction since she'd found a real one. "They're here somewhere, they have to be."

"You need to organize."

"Don't start." She shifted piles aside and kept searching. Damn it. She knew exactly which pile she'd put the advertising material in, but it was gone. Damn, she didn't need yet another problem, another reason for Gwyneth to assume she couldn't handle things. First it had been the out-of-bounds signs, then the bakery order, then the party—it was as if someone was specifically out to cause trouble for her.

She looked at Gwyneth, who was standing in front of her desk with the pinched look to her face that said she was gearing up for another lecture, and knew that she couldn't share her sudden suspicion with her sister—Gwyneth would think she was being ridiculous, passing her own incompetence off on some mysterious prankster. So she started riffling through the papers again. "We need to make a final decision on this stuff, and then decide where to place them. And now that the cafeteria is doing so well, I want to put in separate ads for that in all the Tahoe-area dailies and magazines, as well."

"So you're sleeping with another skier."

Lily's hands went still. "We're talking about the missing ad file."

Gwyneth came close and put her hands over Lily's. "I'm worried about you falling for some ski bum who sees you as his meal ticket to old age."

"Logan is the furthest thing from a ski bum I've ever seen." She pointedly resumed searching for the missing ads. She didn't want to even think about falling for Logan, let alone discuss the possibility out loud—and especially not with either one of her sisters, who could be guaranteed not to understand.

Gwyneth didn't say anything and Lily tried not to look at her, but finally the silence became too heavy and she lifted her head.

"You didn't make a joke or scoff it off," Gwyneth said quietly.

"Scoff what off?"

"The possibility of you falling for him."

"It's only been a few days."

"So say it. Look me in the eyes and say you aren't falling for him."

Damn. Lily looked her right in the eyes, opened her mouth and…nothing came out.

"Good God." Looking shaken, Gwyneth perched a hip on the desk. "Maybe you'd better tell me about him. *All* about him."

"I've got to find that file. If we don't, we miss our placement date. As our accountant, you can't possibly approve of that."

"For once, I am not interested in money. Start talking, Lily."

LOGAN WOKE UP ALONE AND BIT back his disappointment. Apparently fun time was over for Lily, which was fine. After all, in a few days he'd be back in his world, far away from here, living his life, doing what he did best.

And like Lily, he'd be far too busy to lie in bed all morning, no matter how tempting.

He got up, showered, then headed outside. The weather was clear, the previous day's storm long forgotten and he skied for several hours before stopping at the lodge for something hot to drink. He was sitting on the outside deck, which overlooked the terrain park, where the boarders did their tricks, when a shadow fell over him.

Squinting into the bright sunshine, he looked up into a pair of whiskey-colored eyes. Lily smiled and gestured to the spot next to him. "Taken?"

"It is now." He scooted over for her.

She wore boarder pants and a soft white hoodie sweater with the Bay Moon Resort logo on the arm. It zipped to just between her breasts, with two fluffy tassels hanging down. He wondered if she was wearing one of her sexy camisoles beneath, and if her panties matched. "Why did you run off this morning?"

"I didn't." She met his steady gaze and blew out a breath. "Exactly."

He flicked a tassel. "Then what, exactly?"

"I had work."

"Did you get it done?"

"That's a matter of opinion, but I've got a few hours." She looked at him. "To be with you."

Unable to help himself, he touched her jaw and the scratch there from yesterday's rescue. "Then why aren't we still in my bed wrapped around each other, me buried deep inside you, with you panting my name in that sexy little whisper you have?"

She let out a soft, little laugh as the pulse at the base of her throat took off. "Maybe I had something else in mind."

"Like what?"

She lifted a challenging brow. "Scared?"

"Should I be?"

"I can't imagine what I could dish out that would scare you," she said.

"Imagine again, then," he said. "Because everything about you scares me, especially after watching you hang off that cliff yesterday."

Her smile faded.

"No, never mind." He shook his head. "I'm sorry. We both know I'd have done the same thing in a heartbeat, and have more times than I can count. It just seems that when it comes to you, my reasoning seems to fly right out the window."

"Because you care."

"Hell, yeah, I care." He touched her jaw again, his own tight. "More than what makes sense."

She said nothing but covered his hand with her own and held it to her, staring at him for a long moment. Finally, she stood. "Come on."

"Where to?"

She drew him to his feet. "Does it matter?"

He looked down at her and felt his heart tug hard. "Not really."

"Then it's a surprise."

LILY DROVE. "IT'S NOT FAR." She took the narrow, windy mountain road around the back of the lodge. It led into the thick of the woods, where the towering pines blocked out the sun and shrank their world to the inside of her car.

"Where are we?" he asked, enjoying the ride.

"Still on our property, actually." She turned onto another road, which had been plowed only one lane wide, with fifteen-foot-high snow berms on either side.

Logan held on as the road twisted and turned, wondering what they were going to do if they met another car coming in the opposite direction. But thankfully they didn't.

"Here we are." She pulled up to a tiny log cabin with smoke coming out of the chimney and what sounded like an entire pack of dogs barking and howling nearby. "Bring your jacket and gloves." She got out of the car, cupped her hands to her mouth and yelled, "Mary!" and the unseen dogs redoubled their effort. He raised his eyebrows. There wasn't much chance anyone could sneak up on this place.

A woman poked her head out of the cabin and grinned broadly at Lily before she vanished. She appeared a moment later wearing a snowsuit, a beanie and that same grin. "It's a perfect day for this."

"I know," Lily said. "You too busy?"

"I have three reservations, all for later, so you're in luck. Come on." She eyed Logan up and down and then back again. "What, about one-ninety?"

"One seventy-five," Lily said, and the two women exchanged a look and then a grin.

Logan realized they were talking about his weight, and looked curiously to Lily, but she just smiled and led him around the back of the cabin.

There were two long kennels there, filled with what looked like wolves but turned out to be an intriguing mix of huskies and malamutes.

"You ever been dog sledding before?" Mary asked him, as the three of them walked toward a long sled that was sitting between the kennel buildings. The noise level rose even further, accompanied by the dogs trotting around in their individual indoor-outdoor runs, jumping up on the chain-link fences that separated them from the sled and doing a damned good imitation of a bunch of teenagers trying out for a baseball team.

He shook his head. "No, never." A new experience. Rare. "You know, it's like they're all yelling, 'Pick me, pick me.'"

Lily and Mary laughed, and he looked over at Lily. She was smiling at him, excited and happy, and he felt a surge of that himself. Sure, the dog sledding would be a new experience—but so was whatever he was feeling for Lily.

He and Lily paused beside the sled as Mary chose the dogs, speaking quietly to each in turn. She harnessed them one by one, hooking them up to the long leads that were stretched out in the snow in front of the sled. When two of the dogs already harnessed began to bicker, snarling at each other, she quickly stepped between them giving their collars a little shake, and then talking them down.

"They're so eager to go that their energy spills

over," she explained. "And there's always one that wants to better its position in the pack."

"Kind of like people," Lily said, sharing a grin with him that warmed him right through.

As soon as the six dogs were in place, Mary unwrapped the end of the reins from where she'd staked them, holding them tight as the dogs jostled, tails and ears held high, straining against the leather straps.

She handed the reins to Lily, who held them similarly tight. "You know the drill. Enjoy yourselves!"

He and Lily sat on the sled, low to the ground, with Lily's back snug to Logan's front, her hips between his, their legs stretched out in front of them.

Nice, he thought, and wrapped his arms around her, slipping his hands beneath her jacket and sweater and indeed finding another soft camisole. He slipped beneath that, too, and felt the bare skin of her stomach tremble at his touch. Everything within him trembled right along with her.

"Put on your gloves," she said.

"Why?" He let his hands roam, enjoying the way he affected her breathing.

"Trust me," she managed. "You'll need them." She adjusted the reins and said something to the barking, excited dogs, but his mind wasn't on the leisurely dog sled they were about to take, it was on Lily's warm, beautiful body so snug to his, and he slid his hands up and covered her breasts.

Her back arched, her head grinding into his shoulder as she thrust her soft curves into his hands, her nipples boring into his palms while her bottom rocked to his crotch.

Oh, yeah. She wanted him every bit as crazily as he wanted her. This was going to be an extremely nice, leisurely, seductive ride.

Then she yelled a command and the dogs leaped forward, barking like a frenzied wolf pack. The sled jerked into motion, faster than any roller-coaster ride, made all the more stomach-dropping because of their close proximity to the ground, which rushed by Logan's eyes so fast he couldn't even take it all in.

And she just laughed, his fearless warrior. It was all he could do to let go of her breasts and wrap his arms around her, holding on for dear life. "My God, does this thing have brakes?"

"Brakes? We don't need no stinkin' brakes!"

He would have sworn his heart was in his throat as they took the narrow, windy trail, and he gripped her with white knuckles, making her laugh some more.

But truthfully, her joy spilled over, catching him up in her exuberance. With the wind in his face, his arms full of a slim, strong, lovely woman and the emerald forest whipping past them at staggering speeds, he felt his own laughter bubbling up as they climbed the trail.

They came to a small lake, the surface made of smoothest ice, circled on all sides by awe-inspiring peaks. On the north shore was a waterfall, frozen solid. It felt as if they were alone in their very own world.

When Lily steered the dogs onto the frozen water, he held his breath. She slowed down, and all around them a silence reigned, suddenly broken by an earth-shuddering *crack*, which echoed between the mountaintops like bullet fire.

"What the hell?" he gasped.

"It's just the ice cracking."

"Oh, is that all?" His arms tightened on her reflexively, and she turned her head and bit his jaw.

"Scared?" she asked.

Spitless. "Nah."

"Don't worry." She grinned. *Grinned.* "It'll hold us."

"That's good," he managed. "Can we admire this from the shore now?"

"Baby." But she steered them back. Logan didn't let out a slow breath until they were once again on the trail.

"You okay?" she asked.

He slid his cold hands back beneath her clothes. "I am now. How about you?" He plucked at her nipples.

Her hands jerked on the reins but as he well knew, she couldn't possibly let go, so he did it again. "I can't think when you do that," she said unsteadily.

"Thinking is overrated." And again… "Feel out of control?"

"Y-yes."

"Good." He bit her ear. "Now you know how it feels."

She wriggled her butt, the motion having a desperate feel to it. He slid one hand down her tummy and between her thighs, loving the sound that ripped out of her.

"Keep us on the road," he said gently when she started to lose track of the reins. Then he pressed his fingers against her.

"Ohmigod."

"The tree, Lily. Watch the tree."

She managed to steer them clear but let out a strangled sound of desire and a shiver when he slid his fingers inside her loose pants.

"Warm enough?" he asked, dipping beneath her panties to find hot, wet flesh that made him groan.

"I don't think I'll ever be cold again," she managed.

One hand between her legs, the other up her shirt, wanting her so badly he couldn't see straight, he looked around them for a place to stop.

She let out a choked laugh and took them back to the small cabin. As they climbed out of the sled Lily handed the reins back to Mary, thanking her with a hug. Once out of Mary's hearing, she nudged him with her shoulder. "You were thinking we could get a little action out there."

"We got a little action."

"I meant *real* action." Her eyes were filled with wicked intent as she danced a single finger down his chest and hooked it into the loose waistband of his ski pants.

He was already so hard he could have pounded nails into steel.

She leaned into him. "I know one more thing we can do out here…"

Yes.

"Follow me…" And she backed away from him, still giving him that mind-blowing smile that promised him the moon, then she turned and ran around the corner of the cabin.

She was crazier than he. They couldn't go out there and just— It was cold. Someone would see—

Ah, hell. He loped after her, turning the corner and—

Took a snowball directly in the face.

The icy ball fell apart on impact, dripping little shards of snow down his face and into his collar. Shocked, frozen on the spot, he blinked the ice off his lashes and stared at her.

She clapped her hands over her mouth, which didn't hold her laugh in.

"Lily?"

"Yes?" she asked around her gloved fingers.

"You're going to want to run now," he said silkily, pulling on his gloves and bending to scoop up a handful of ammunition, careful not to pat it together too tightly.

With a laughing scream, she whirled and ran, but he easily beaned her in the back.

Her mistake was that she stopped, laughing as she glanced at him over her shoulder.

He caught her, tumbled her to the snow, a wriggling, screeching, desperate-to-escape woman, and with a grin, he held her down with one hand to her chest, using his other to sprinkle snow in her face.

Then he let her escape.

She crawled away a few steps, then turned back to him, taunting. "Is that the worst you can do?" She grabbed more snow, chucked it at him, and then when he bent for a handful, took off running.

Once more he caught her, mostly because she let him, and again, he took them both down to the snow, capturing her wrists this time, hauling them above her head, holding her captive while he tugged down the zipper of her jacket, spread it wide open.

"Logan," she warned, her breasts heaving with

each laughing breath. Her nipples were hard, pressing against the material of her sweater, begging for his touch, which he planned to give. "Don't you dare—"

He stuffed a handful of snow down her sweater and then patted the material.

She squealed and he bent his head, taking her frozen mouth in his. It heated instantly, and opened to him. He absorbed her soft moan and matched it with one of his own as their tongues, hot in comparison to the rest of them, slid together. Still restrained by his hand, hers flexed, and she arched up into him. Oh, yeah, he loved that, and he lifted his head long enough to tug his glove off with his teeth. He cupped her face with his bare hand now and whispered her name.

Her body writhed against his, and he let her hands go to gather her even closer. She opened her legs to accommodate his hips, and he rocked them to her, going even harder at her harsh breathing, at the un-focused, needy glaze in her eyes. They were out of control and he didn't care.

She yanked off her gloves, too, then stuck her hands down the back of his ski pants, beneath his shorts, making him yelp at her frozen fingers. Laughing, he surged up on his knees, pulling her up, as well, his ass now frozen solid, along with another essential part of him. "Not here."

"Where, then?" She looked over her shoulder at the cabin, and he wasn't so far gone that he couldn't see her trying to figure out where. Now.

He laughed again and shook his head. He wanted *warm*, thank you very much. "I'll give you two choices. Your room or mine."

THEY WENT TO HIS, AND LOGAN had barely gotten Lily inside before he stripped her out of her clothes. His, too, and though she tried to touch, he pulled her into his shower. She wanted him beyond belief, beyond thoughts, knowing only that it wasn't just the hot water beading down on them that was restoring feeling to her extremities.

Her eyes drifted shut while he soaped her up, murmuring in her ear the whole time, telling her exactly what he was going to do to her as soon as she warmed up.

"But I'm warm now," she whispered shamelessly, and wrapped her fingers around his erection.

"Here, then," he said with a shudder. Backing her up to the wall, he lifted her and thrust home, making her come instantly. *Instantly.* Then, before she could get over the shock of that or even float back to herself, he kissed he, and, using the tile as leverage, took her hard and fast, bringing her to another screaming orgasm before he let himself go.

Afterward, with her body still trembling, he carried her to his bed and started again, slow and dreamy and seductive this time, until her breath sobbed in her throat, his name tumbling over and over from her lips, her heart both aching and pounding.

And it still wasn't enough.

AN HOUR LATER SHE MADE IT to her office feeling a little bit like the naughty schoolgirl caught sneaking late into class. At least all of her tension had been released by some seriously mind-blowing orgasms. *Thank you, Logan.*

Debbie was sitting on her desk, filing her nails. "Look who the cat dragged in."

Carrie came in and set a huge stack on her desk, then blew a strand of hair from her eyes. "Sorry, babe. But you've got to go through that."

Debbie looked smug. "Ha."

Lily sighed. "Is it all stuff you and I have discussed?"

"Mostly," Carrie said.

"Then you can split it with me." Lily divided the stack in half and got down to it, thinking it couldn't take that long. She'd be back outside in no time. "Did you find the missing ad file?" she asked Carrie, hoping that whoever had messed with the file had merely moved it, rather than actually taken it.

Debbie fingered the messy desk. "How can you find anything?"

"Do you have a reason for being here?" Lily asked.

"Yep." Debbie hopped down. "To offer my help."

"That's funny."

"I mean it. I want to help."

"Fine. You can help me find the ad."

"Okeydokey."

But they couldn't find it anywhere. Damn it. Starting over would take forever and cost them a late penalty. If they didn't get into the trade magazines, they could lose potential business for next year. "I know it's here…"

"Lose something else?" Gwyneth came into the office and perched a hip on the corner of her desk. She reached out to unbutton and then rebutton the blouse

Lily had put on incorrectly only a few minutes before when she'd run to her room for dry clothing. "Someone's been dressing in a hurry. A nooner today with the ski bum?"

"Jealous?"

"You know, given the wattage of your smile, I just might be."

"Good. And I told you, he's not a ski bum."

"You keep defending him, little sis, and I'm going to get even more worried. Oh, and don't worry about finding the ads now. Deadline passed. We lost the opportunity to be in any California trade mags next season."

"I had those ads done. They vanished."

"If that makes you feel better."

"What would make me feel better is you out of my face."

As Gwyneth disappeared in a huff, Lily dived into work.

No ads meant they'd have to work extra hard to reach the trade markets next year, which meant extra work for her. This was beyond just a trick—it could hurt the lodge's profits. And if it wasn't some totally weird, out-of-this-world coincidence, if it was the same person who'd removed the out-of-bounds signs…

Hell, they were lucky no one had injured themselves, or worse.

She was going to be keeping her eyes wide open from now on, watching for anything remotely suspicious—and she had her patrollers doing the same, only she'd justified it to them by using the sign incident. For now, though, she had a stack of work to get through and a damn good incentive to get it done. She and Logan had arranged to meet for a late-night walk on the frozen pond to the east of the resort, and as she worked, she watched the clock. At the right time, she left the office and made her way outside.

And when she saw him waiting for her, leaning against a tree with that long, leanly muscled body she knew every inch of now, the tension shifted again, into a sexual pull, a desperate need, and a softening of the heart.

Oh, boy. Gwyneth was right, she *was* in trouble. Big trouble.

Because she *was* falling for him.

Or at least her body was.

Not her brain, though. No, her brain was far too smart for that.

12

THEY TOOK A MIDNIGHT WALK beneath a full moon that hung over them like a magic ball, casting and reflecting a white glow over the snow and ice around them, making Logan feel once again as if they were alone in the world, just him and Lily.

"Up there." She pointed to a small outcropping to the east of the lodge, thick with snow. Below was a deep basin of more rocks and snow. "If we can climb up there, the view is incredible."

He eyed the hill, sharp with rocks and what was sure to be ice and powder, and slowly shook his head. "It's a death trap. We'll slide, all the way to the bottom."

Which, he didn't point out, he couldn't even see.

"It's safer than it looks. Believe me, I've done it. I wouldn't be stupid out here. Chicken?"

He craned his neck and eyed the climb, then Lily. She was bundled up in a thick jacket against the night's chill, hood up, with only her face showing and a cocky grin curving her mouth. "*Chicken?*"

She flapped her hands and made the unmistakable squawk of a hen. He'd never backed down from a dare or a rescue or anything dangerous in his life, but he had to laugh because this woman made him want to do just that. Back down. Keep her safe.

Obviously he was losing his mind. She didn't need anyone to keep her safe.

Or to fall for her the way he suspected he was beginning to.

Yes, definitely, he was losing it. Something he was all the more sure of when he actually climbed up to the peak with her. They were both huffing and puffing by the time they got there, and damp with the snow, not to mention freezing, but at the top, he went still at the sight sprawled out in front of them. Above them, the moon lay low and full and stunning, lighting a vast, softly glowing valley surrounded by sharp, sky-scraping mountains. "My God."

"I know. I never get tired of the view." Awed, turning in a slow circle, she took it all in.

"Me, either," he said, not taking his eyes off her.

She turned to him and touched his face as she smiled. "Do you mean to make me melt?"

"Just a bonus." He pulled her toward him for a kiss, but one taste wasn't enough, and the next thing he knew, they were leaning against each other, panting with need. "Now," she demanded, and all but dragged him down the mountain and back to her room, where he gladly ravished and cherished her body with his, with everything he had, the cliff and the view forgotten as he struggled to hold back the words and emotions that suddenly wanted to fly from his mouth. When they'd both come explosively, they lay back, gasping for breath.

Naked, damp and looking quite sated, Lily sat up.

Logan groaned and rolled to his stomach, oddly exhausted. Lily shoved her hair from her face and slapped him playfully on the ass. "Your body is so hot. I just want to gobble you right up."

He didn't move a muscle. Couldn't. "If you're looking for round two, I need a second."

"Actually...I was wondering something."

He could hear the hesitation in her voice—this from a woman who never hesitated which made his stomach sink. Had he said something in the moment, something stupid and unforgettable? Gathering his strength, he lifted his head and looked at her.

"I was just wondering why you always seem to look out for me," she said softly.

"What?"

She ran a finger down his spine and sighed. "Seriously. I just want to bite you. Why, Logan?"

"Why do you want to bite me?"

"Why do you look out for me?" She sat cross-legged at his hip and dug her fingers into the knotted muscles at his shoulders. This ripped a groan of pleasure from his throat. "I should have offered you a massage before now," she murmured, massaging the kinks left by days of hard skiing and wild sex. "You've given me one. You've hung out with me at the rescues, skied with me whenever you could, taken care of me both in and out of bed...." She sighed.

"What's the matter? Hard to keep it just light and fun?" he asked, giving her back her own words.

Her fingers went still for a telling moment. "Yes, if you must know, because with you, Logan, it's not just light and fun. It's more." She sounded baffled. "And I guess what I'm asking is why go to all this trouble, why hook me in like this when you're leaving in two days?"

In her voice he could hear the worry, the angst that she'd kept from him until now, and it moved him enough to temper the frustration her words caused. He wasn't the only one who was struggling to keep it light and easy. She was in, her heart was in, and it scared her. Feeling unexpectedly tender, he rolled over, slid his arms around her and pulled her over on top of him.

Her gaze met his, waiting. Only problem, he didn't have a ready answer. All his life he'd taken care of others. Truthfully, it seemed like second nature to him. Now there was Lily, a woman more than capable of taking care of herself, more so than anyone he'd ever met. That in itself was incredibly refreshing, and also terrifyingly attractive to him. He didn't have to take care of her, she could do it herself.

And yet he wanted to. Wanted to keep her safe and happy. Always. A seriously worrying thought, because his life wasn't conducive to a relationship, much less a long-distance one.

She was staring down at him, trying to read his thoughts. He slid his hands up her spine, sank his fingers in her hair. "You think it's trouble to want you? To want to take care of you?"

"You're leaving in two days." She sat up, straddling his hips with her bare legs. "I guess what I'm saying is don't forget that."

He cupped a breast, skimming his thumb over her

nipple, loving how her breathing changed, how her body reacted for him. "I won't forget." And if for long moments he did just that, he'd deal with it, because she was right. This was enough, it had to be. Knowing it, he pulled her down for a long, deep kiss, his heart kicking into gear at the feel of her soft, supple, nude body against his.

When she lifted her head again, her eyes were heavy and filled with heat. "Are you trying to shut me up?"

He gripped her thighs, opening them farther, groaning at the feel of her wet, creamy heat gliding over his growing erection. "No. You can keep talking."

"Okay, because I— *Oh*. Oh, yeah…" she murmured as he eased inside her. Her eyes closed, her head fell back as her hips rocked to his. "I forgot what I wanted to say."

"That's okay, too," he said, and let her take him.

On Logan's second-to-last day a snowstorm hit. Luckily for Lily, Chris ended up short-staffed, so she used that as an opportunity to work ski patrol in the morning. Logan skied along with her. After lunch, she had to get back to the office. Logan walked her there, kissing her goodbye—a kiss that led to her dragging him into her bathroom and enjoying the body she could not seem to get enough of.

Afterward, she staggered to her desk with a grin on her face. She had to attend several nap-inducing meetings, one for guest services and one for accounting. The first ended with Sara moody and teary, the other with Gwyneth demanding and critical. Aunt

Debbie attended each as a member of the board of directors—a position Lily's grandmother had given her to keep her in the loop but not actually in charge of anything. She sat back, looking quite pleased with herself and her lack of responsibilities.

It drove Lily crazy. The meetings turned into one long excuse to be critical of her efforts, and the lost ad file gave her sisters plenty of ammunition. Since they didn't believe that she'd actually drafted the ads in the first place, she figured that revealing her suspicion that someone was messing with her on purpose was totally useless. Besides, who could she possibly point her finger at? One of them? They might think she was incompetent, but neither of them would sabotage her on purpose. A disgruntled staff member? But she knew every single staff member, in the lodge and on the hill, and none of them fit the bill, either. Most of them had worked for the resort for years, and those that hadn't had been screened. No one had been fired lately, or even disciplined.

Could it be an unhappy customer? She'd certainly annoyed the hell out of those two identical twins who'd been fighting, but they wouldn't have the access they needed to her office—or the brains needed to pull off a sustained effort like this. She was drawing a blank on suspects and motives and frankly, if she wasn't being targeted personally, she'd have trouble believing it herself.

The glow of wild, animal sex long gone, Lily did her best to put them all out of her thoughts. By that evening, she was chomping at the bit. She'd promised Logan she'd meet up with him at the bar. Already late thanks to another computer crisis, she ran through the cafeteria and got caught by a frantic Carl, who had a hot date and needed help with cleanup. Sighing, she grabbed two large bags of trash and walked down the long driveway around the back of the bar and cafeteria. Lugging a bag in each hand, she admired the dark night around her as big fluffy snowflakes fell from the sky, thick as a soft, gauzy white blanket, utterly silent.

Walking alone, with the lights of the resort behind her, only a flashlight tucked under her arm for guidance, bobbing a thin beam of light up and down, she felt chilled on the outside but dreamy and sated on the inside, thinking about the night ahead.

She'd enjoyed their eight minutes in her office bathroom. She probably still had the faucet impressions in her butt from where he'd pressed her back while he'd pounded himself into her, but then again, he most likely had her fingernail impressions in his.

In the dark, quiet night, she grinned, and then laughed. God, he made her feel good. Sexy and shameless, too, and that was a little scary because he was out of here soon—but suddenly that wasn't nearly as scary as the big lump that rose between her and the Dumpster. The big lump that suddenly stood up on its back paws and towered over her.

A big bear the size of a small VW Bug.

Oh, shit. *Shit*. All the bear rules flew through her head as the flashlight hit the ground, bouncing once before extinguishing itself. *Don't whirl and run*, she told herself in the dark. *Don't scream. Don't look aggressive*.

But it was one thing to remember the bear rules,

another entirely to follow them in a calm, clear manner when there was a bear looking at her, licking its chops. Oh, God. She dropped the trash bags.

And though she couldn't see clearly, she imagined the bear made eye contact, held it.

She didn't blink. Hell, she didn't breathe. In the dark came a low grumbling. A growl. Her stomach dropped, her entire body went rigid. She'd run into bears before. Once she'd seen a mama bear and her two cubs, but from a nice, cozy distance. Another time she'd been hiking and had nearly stumbled over a big brown bear lying right in the center of the walk, sprawled on his back, the sun on his belly. He'd tipped his head back and studied her from his upside-down pose, a look on his face that said, *It's your lucky day, lady, 'cause I'm too fat and lazy to come eat you.*

But this bear didn't seem fat and lazy. He'd rumbled to his feet quickly, as if she'd startled him, which was the last thing one ever wanted to do to a bear. Now he stood only a few feet from her, close enough to take a good swipe at her with a massive paw.

"Hey, big guy. You want the trash? Take it." She nudged it closer with her foot. "Here."

He didn't move, not a twitch, putting them at an impasse she'd never wanted. "I'm just going to go away now." She lifted a foot to take a backward step, but another rough growl erupted from his throat and she froze.

Her heart was pounding so loudly she was surprised he didn't cover his ears in pain.

He took a step toward her, snapping his teeth at her, a sign of aggression.

Despite the frigid night, she felt sweat trickle down her spine. Close as she was, she could see his sharp canines glowing. His mouth was watering. She imagined he had bad breath from his last victim.

She didn't want to be his next one, she really, really didn't. Even as crazy as her world got sometimes, hanging off a cliff trying to make a rescue, for example, she rarely thought about dying.

She thought about it now, about the things she'd miss. The lodge. Her friends. Her sisters, crazy as that seemed.

She'd miss her last night with Logan. She'd miss that a lot.

A loud metal-on-metal noise clanged through the air, and the bear jerked. Lily jerked, too, but the sound kept coming. Someone was banging, trying to scare the bear off for her. The large animal craned its head away from her and she used the opportunity to take another step backward, not daring to whirl and run yet.

The clanging grew louder, accompanied by a shout.

The bear started, then began moving quickly, lumbering right past Lily, so close she felt his snow-covered fur brush her arm and leg.

And then he was gone.

She didn't remember sinking to the snow, but that's where she was when Logan hit his knees in front of her. "Lily. My God, he was huge. Are you okay?" Without waiting for her to answer, his arms came around her hard.

She discovered another thing she'd miss—his hands on her. She'd miss that a lot, too. "Was that you making that noise?"

"Yes."

"I'm okay."

"I'm not. Hold on to me a minute."

She could feel his heart pounding hard, or maybe that was hers. In either case, she did as he'd asked and held on. In fact, she considered never letting go.

From behind them came voices now, where before there'd been only eerie silence. A handful of people rushed toward them, led by Matt.

"Tell me the whole lodge didn't see that," she said.

Matt crouched beside them and tugged on a strand of her hair. "Just a few guests, and they're still inside."

"I think he's gone."

"Yeah."

"I'm glad he's not busy eating you."

"Because you'd miss me?"

"Because you'd have given him indigestion."

"Ha ha."

Sara pushed in beside Matt and threw herself and her big old belly right at Lily, who just barely managed to catch her. "Oh, my God, Lily Rose! You were nearly eaten alive!"

Lily patted her sister's bump. "Don't get too excited, I'm still here."

Then Gwyneth pushed her way through. "Heard you were almost bear bait," she said, toughlike, then folded like a cheap suitcase as she sank to the snow and hugged Lily hard. "You enjoy giving me gray hair, don't you?"

"I live for it. Sorry you didn't inherit tonight."

Gwyneth looked around at the resort and sighed.

"Yeah. Next time make sure to scare a hungrier bear, could you?" Then she hugged Lily again, hard.

Aunt Debbie joined them. "Look at you, front and center, as usual."

"Yeah, I'm so desperate for attention, I asked that bear to meet me at the trash bin."

"You didn't ask to be Grandma's sole heir either, but that's what happened."

Lily's smile faded. "True enough."

Gwyneth, either oblivious or trying to relieve the sudden tension, sighed at the scene. "Would you look at the mess?"

One of the two garbage bags had ripped, spilling some of its contents onto the ground, already getting covered with snow. And yet it wasn't the bear or their guests on Lily's mind now.

It was Aunt Debbie and her quiet resentment. Gwyneth and her not-so-quiet resentment.

And the fact that Lily herself felt a sudden and nearly overwhelming resentment toward them all. She looked into Logan's warm, concerned eyes and shook her head to his silent question. She was fine. She always was.

But for the first time in her life, it wasn't the mountain making her fine. No, a man was doing that.

A man who was leaving tomorrow.

13

LOGAN WATCHED Lily gather all her family and staff back inside, asking them to reassure the guests, who were watching from behind the safety of the windows of the bar and common room. "Just in case the big bastard comes back," she told him quietly. "Don't want anyone else to become bear dinner, either."

Seeing the strain in her expression, he stroked a hand up her back. He didn't think it was the bear incident, but rather whatever had flickered between her and her sister and aunt. "You hanging in?"

"Yeah." She leaned into him for a moment. "So what were you making that noise with? The one that scared him off?"

"Matt told me you'd gone out. He gave me his flashlight. When I saw you and the bear at a standoff, I banged it on the recycling bins behind you."

She smiled. "Quick thinking." Then she pressed her face into his shirt and inhaled, as if he was better than air.

"You weren't so bad yourself." His hand came up and cupped her head, holding her close when she might have pulled back. "Cool, calm, just like always. Do you ever panic?"

"I was plenty panicked. I just didn't want to be munched on by a bear, that's all." She lifted her head and smiled. "I'd better remind everyone to be careful out there."

He watched her move through the common room, running her world in her usual love-me-as-I-am way, joking and sweetly sarcastic yet firm and in charge.

And utterly unaware of the fact he couldn't take his eyes off her.

Tonight would be their last night, and he had no idea if she even realized it. He'd thought to leave the lodge without regrets, but it turned out he had one big one.

Leaving her.

How many times had he promised her that this thing was for fun only? He'd be lying if he gave her that promise now, tonight. It'd been a good long time since he'd felt the urge to put a woman through the stress of fitting into his life, but now he could admit that maybe he hadn't wanted to put himself through it, either. At the moment, he couldn't remember why.

Near the roaring fire, Lily sat perched on the edge of the couch, chatting and laughing with a handful of guests. She tossed her head back when she laughed, giving it her all. She always gave her all.

And yet she'd held back with him, big-time.

But he'd held back, too. Now they had only one night left, and he didn't want to hold back anything. Needing their last few hours all to himself, he walked over to her, drew her up and brought her fingers to his mouth.

Her eyelashes fluttered down over her eyes, but

not before he saw the surprise and pleasure flickering there. "What can I do for you, Mr. Logan White?"

"Anything you want," he murmured in her ear. "As long as you're naked."

A blush rose over her cheeks, which he found not only adorable but also an unbearable turn-on, given all they'd done. He didn't touch her other than her hand, and that in itself teased him into an erection. "And wet," he added in a barely-there whisper. "I want you really wet."

"Excuse me," she said to the guests, grabbing his hand and taking him into the office wing, then past that to her apartment. They kept stopping to kiss, to whisper breathless promises, to touch and tease some more, until Logan could hardly breathe.

At her door, she stopped to search her pockets for her key while he used the opportunity to step up close behind her and cup her breasts, stroke her nipples.

"Stop that." She sounded breathless as she fumbled with the key, trying to get it into the lock.

"Really?" He tugged at the tight, taut peaks. "You want me to stop?"

"Okay, don't even think about it." She closed her eyes and pressed her bottom back, grinding into his crotch. "Don't you dare."

There was no one in the dimly lit hallway. Smiling against her neck, he slid his hands down her back, squeezed her squeezable ass and dipped his fingers between her thighs.

She dropped her forehead to her door and arched back into him. "Please," she gasped. "Help me get us inside."

Instead, he went beneath her sweater and another soft camisole to cup her bare breasts while he scraped his teeth over the side of her neck.

"Oh." She trembled, a reaction that brought out more heat and added a shocking amount of tenderness to the mix, as well. "Logan, I...I can't open the door."

He skimmed his thumbs over her nipples again, and she dropped the key.

"Uh-oh," he tsked. "Better get that."

When she bent for it, he gripped her waist and rocked his hips to her ass. She moaned and whipped around, shoving the key at him. The moment he got the door open, she dragged him inside, slammed the door, then pushed him back against it, biting his throat as she tore at his shirt. "Hurry. Now."

He'd wanted to take this slow, but he was fired up now, hungry and desperate. Shaking with it. She got his shirt halfway unbuttoned and off his shoulders, trapping his arms while she went to work on his pants.

"Lily—" The word clogged in his throat along with his breath when she wrapped her hand around his erection and stroked. Then she dropped to her knees, freed him completely and took him in her mouth.

Staggering back against the closed door, all he managed was a groan. He shrugged out of his shirt and sank his fingers into her hair, dying when she swirled her tongue around the tip of him. Hauling her up, he swallowed her protest with his mouth. "We want to make this last more than two seconds," he said, and tossed her to the bed, coming down on top of her, pinning her hands with his to hold her wriggling, gorgeous body still as he slowly removed her shirt and camisole—sunshine-yellow this time—absorbing her low moans of pleasure when he tasted each new section of skin he exposed. Then he clamped his mouth on her breast and sucked hard. She slid her fingers into his hair and arched up, giving him better access as she wrapped her legs around his hips, trying to rock against him.

"Not fast this time." He shuddered when she rocked again, but somehow found the strength to hold back. "I'm going to take you slowly, damn it." He licked her nipple, then blew on the wet peak. "*Very* slowly. And you're going to let me. You're going to watch."

"Logan—" Under him, she writhed, her hands in his hair still fisted tightly, her belly quivering as he made his way down her torso, her ribs, nipping her as he went, soothing the little love bites with his tongue. When he got to her ski pants, he unfastened them, kissed the bare skin he found there beneath her belly button and then tugged the pants off her hips, exposing yellow satin panties. *Wet* yellow satin panties. With a groan, he lowered those, too, and stroked a finger over the trimmed, soft hair between her thighs.

Beneath him, she fought to open her legs, but the pants and panties at her thighs kept her captive. "Logan, *please*."

"I will please," he promised and swept his tongue over her, into her.

Whatever she'd been about to say caught in her throat as again he danced his tongue across her, and then again and again, until she began to come.

And still he stroked her with his tongue, slowly now, bringing her down with soft kisses until her muscles trembled wildly but loosely, until she let go of her tight fistfuls of the sheets at her sides. He rose up to his knees, removed her pants and lifted her hips, spreading her so that he could sink in deep.

A total and complete homecoming, he thought, as her moan melded with his. He cupped her face, sank his fingers into her hair, loving that she didn't close her eyes but met his as they took each other, fast now, hard, too, gasping with each thrust, letting out wordless demands and cries of pleasure as they breathed each other's air. There was a look in her whiskey eyes that gripped his heart and held on as she cried out and began to come again, freeing him. He watched her go over as fiercely as she did everything in her life, her eyes open and opaque on his, shattering with utter abandon, taking him with her. Always taking him with her.

MUCH LATER, THEY TOOK A SHOWER together. Lily took great pleasure in Logan's long, leanly muscled body, all wet and gleaming.

Luckily for her, he appeared to feel the same way. His soap-covered hands ran over her shoulders, digging into the knots there, then dallied at her breasts, tugging lightly on her nipples, making her knees wobble. "We'll kill each other," she murmured, and he laughed softly.

"Yeah, but what a way to go."

He had her there. His magic hands turned her away from him, lifting her arms to the tile wall at about shoulder height. "Stay," he whispered in her ear and glided his hands down her spine, over her buttocks, down her legs and then back up again, between her thighs now.

Already halfway to orgasm from the feel of his big, warm, soapy hands stroking her drenched body, she thrust back against him, the breath sawing in and out of her lungs, thinking, *Now, now, now, please now.*

"Mmm, I love your body, Lily."

"Just don't stop."

"I don't intend to." As the water rained over them, washing away the soap, he nibbled at the back of her thigh, lightly bit the curve of her butt, all while playing her with those hot, knowing fingers. She strained toward him, both perplexed and furious that he could so effortlessly hold her there on the edge. "Damn it, Logan."

Surging up, he whipped her around, pressing her between the cold tile wall and his hot, wet body to thrust himself home. "I want you." Chest heaving, he pressed his jaw to hers. "I always want you, it's never enough."

Never was a terrifying word, and the right one, and all her temper drained. "I know. *I know.*" Steam rose around them so she had to blink to see him clearly as she cupped his face.

Eyes fierce and impossibly dark, his broad shoulders and back protecting her from the pounding water, he began to move, gripping her hips with his hands as he destroyed her with long, hard strokes. He took her mouth, pulling back only to whisper her name, just her name, and from inside an emotion banked, swelled as he emptied himself into her. And with pleasure and need and love spreading to burst within her, she followed him over.

14

LOGAN WOKE UP TO SOMEONE swearing like a sailor. Lily. She tossed her walkie-talkie to a chair and stalked the length of the room naked. From what he gathered, the weather was the "son of a bitch."

He sat up and looked outside. Pure white, halfway up the windows. "Wow."

"It surprised everyone," she said. "Even the weather forecasters. We've got harsh winds, heavy drifts of up to four feet over the icy snow we already had. Of course, the two days' worth of sun we had first didn't help—fresh snow over ice is never good." She came back to the bed and shook her head, looking lean and toned and beautiful. "It's rare, but we're shut down. Totally shut down. Now I've got patrollers worrying about avalanches, people whining about not being able to get here, a chef freaking out because the food didn't get delivered, guests not able to get out—" She broke off and looked at him as it dawned on her—he was one of those people who wouldn't be able to get out. "We'll get you to your flight," she said quickly, and began shimmying into a pair of pants. "Don't worry." She wasn't looking at him now, instead getting dressed as fast as she could.

With a sigh, he got out of the bed and went to her. She stared at his throat, then ran her finger over the skin there. "I left a mark," she said softly. "I bit you and left a mark."

"Then I'll have something to remember you by."

Her face went carefully blank.

He tried to draw her close but she danced back, shaking her head as she finished getting dressed.

"No regrets, right?" She smiled. "Just fun. Look, I've got to go. I have to get out there."

"I can help."

"No, you've done too much for us. For me."

"Maybe I like to." Again, he tried to pull her close but she was having none of it.

"I'll let you know when you can get out." She grabbed her shoes and shut the door behind her.

"So brave." He sank to the bed and pulled on his clothes. "And such a damn coward at the same time." One last time, he looked around at Lily's bedroom, at the rumpled bed where they'd made love. Everything inside him ached, but he left the room without looking back.

In the common room, a fire warmed the hearth. People milled around, talking softly in the early morning, staring out the windows in disbelief at the amount of snow that had fallen the night before.

The light outside had shifted from a dark predawn glow to a sort of gauzy gray light as the sun strained but failed to get through the layer of clouds and snow.

Gwyneth was there, moving through toward the offices with a clipboard in her hand. He stopped her. "Can I help?"

Looking a little frazzled, she managed a smile. "Can you get Mother Nature to take a nap? No? Then just enjoy."

He pulled on his jacket and headed outside. There he found Lily organizing a crew to clear the walkways and parking lot. Much to her dismay, he grabbed a shovel. "Hey," she said, already shaking her head. "You don't need to—"

"Stop it. I'm here. I'm helping."

She stared at him for a long moment, then apparently decided she couldn't change his mind, and they all got to work. It took hours, removing snow as it continued to come down. They didn't talk, they couldn't, there was no opportunity. But Logan was painfully aware that if it hadn't been for the storm, he'd have been already gone.

By midday, they finally began to get ahead of the snowfall. Exhausted and starving, they took a break for lunch.

Sitting in the cafeteria at a couple of long tables, they all consumed mass quantities of calories to refuel after the heavy work. Lily sat at the table with a clipboard, dividing up new assignments, when Sara came waddling through. Lily lifted her head and glared at her sister. "Why the hell are you here?"

"Last I checked, I work here." Sara smiled, but sighed when Lily didn't give. "Okay, so we never left last night. After Matt's shift, the snow was already too bad, so we just stayed over. Don't worry, Mama, I didn't go out in this."

"See that you don't." Lily pointed at her belly.

"And don't even think about going into labor, do you hear me?"

"Aye, aye, Captain!"

"I mean it, Sara."

"So do I." Because Lily was still just scowling at her, Sara moved in and hugged her tight. "Don't worry, no delivering any babies for you, not today. You have enough to worry about with people stuck trying to get here, or stuck trying to get out, Aunt Debbie included. Matt's worried about getting his supplies. Oh, and speaking of my husband, do you know where he is?"

Lily looked over the faces at the table and frowned. "He was helping clear snow, and then said something about Debbie wanting a snowmobile ride. I'll check."

"Don't worry, I'll radio them."

When she'd gone, Lily used her phone to get the latest weather report, then stood up and addressed her staff. "Okay, listen up. The highways are still closed, including the 80 from the summit to Verdi. Snow's still coming down, obviously, thick and wet. Sierra cement, our favorite. According to the radar, we should get a break in an hour or so for a while, enough to open the 80 for a bit, anyway." She looked at Logan, and he knew she was thinking about him getting to the airport. "At that time, people will be able to get out, and the new guests in. Expect mass confusion and grumpiness from all corners."

"Even yours?"

Lily lifted a brow at Chris. "Want a double shift?"

"Jeez, just kidding." Chris lowered his cap and went back to shoveling in food.

Lily pushed away her untouched tray and moved to leave, but Logan grabbed her hand. "Come on, sit down and eat."

"I'm too busy—"

"Eat." Not taking no for an answer, he tugged her down next to him and put her tray back in front of her.

On the pretense of stroking back a strand of hair, he outlined her ear with his finger. She'd run a Sno-Cat today, operated a huge snowblower and shoveled as much snow as he had. "You're pushing yourself pretty hard."

A shoulder jerked. "Not really."

"Lily."

Her eyes closed a moment, and then she looked at him, really looked at him, and he saw what he'd been looking for. A devastating flash of emotion that would have brought him to his knees if he'd been standing. "Ah, Lily—"

"Don't," she whispered furiously. "Damn it, don't say a word or I'll lose it. I mean it." She shoved another bite in and looked straight ahead as she chewed, chasing the food down with his water. Then she shoved the tray back and stood. "Let's go, ace. We have more snow removal to do."

He figured that was the only invitation he was going to get to stick close. Together they took one of the Sno-Cats and worked on clearing the closed section of the entrance road. Inside the cat, they were high above the ground, in two bucket seats, surrounded by controls that he knew nothing about but that Lily worked as if she'd been born to it. The air was warm and close, the heater blasting, the windows half-fogged. They stripped out of their jackets and gloves, then Lily went back to working the controls with the same quiet, fierce intensity with which she'd made love to him only hours before.

"You know, much as you keep clearing, it's going to keep falling," he said lightly, hoping for a smile.

She just shot him a long glance before going back to clearing as if her life depended on it. They'd already rescued no less than six stranded cars and were working on clearing the parking lot to unstrand a whole bunch more when the radio chirped with word that the 80 had just opened and wasn't expected to stay that way for long.

"This is your chance to get out," she said to the window.

Outside, the snow had stopped falling, for now, but everything around them—the roads, the trees, the signs—was a solid, frozen white wonderland, clear and ice-cold. Lily pulled to a hut in the parking lot, and though she hit the brake, she did not turn off the cat. "Better hurry." There was a hint of impatience in her voice.

He looked at her, astonished. "You want me to hurry and leave?"

"You have a flight, damn it. You need to go. *Now.* I cleared a path for your rental car."

"So this whole damn thing, the whole last six hours of mind-numbing work and effort, was so that you could get me out?"

"Yes."

He was stunned.

"Well, what's so strange about that? You have to go."

"Yeah, I do. You know, I figure there's two possible reasons for this. You're either tired of me…" She didn't move, didn't even blink. "…or you're more terrified of what we've shared than I thought."

She stared at him for another beat, then turned straight ahead again, giving away nothing except the fact she was chewing on her lower lip. "This is a bad time to discuss this."

"*Scared*," he decided, lifting a brow when she whipped her head to him, piercing him with a look.

"I'm not." She said this through her teeth. "I've told you, nothing scares me."

Uh-huh. Except, he was guessing, anything that even remotely resembled matters of the heart. *Well, welcome to the club, sweetheart.* He hadn't been lonely before he'd met her, and hadn't felt particularly unfulfilled.

But even after just a week with this woman, he knew he'd been changed forever. "Something this good isn't worth doing only halfway, Lily." The words and the intent behind them no longer surprised him. Having feelings for someone didn't have to be a burden.

Not with someone like Lily.

"Tell me you haven't forgotten this was just for fun," she said.

"Why? So you can walk away from this, no regrets? Just chalk it up to another fun time had by all?"

"Logan…what choice do we have?"

"There are always choices. Always," he said softly, looking right at her, through her, to the scared woman inside. "All you have to do is want it bad enough. Deep down you know that, you've lived like that. *Lily*." Squeezing her fingers with his, he reached up and touched her face with his free hand. "I don't want to let this go."

She squeezed her eyes shut, then opened them. "It's only been a week."

"Exactly. I want more. Let's go with this thing, see where it takes us."

"You're going back to Ohio. A very long way away."

"That's not a good enough reason to walk away."

"It is for me." And she hopped out of the cat.

LILY TOOK TWO STEPS OUT OF the cat, sank deep into the snow up to her thighs, swore lavishly, then got back into the machine and met Logan's gaze. He didn't want to let this go, she thought in panic. Oh, my God, he really didn't. "This is crazy. *Stupid*."

She marveled at that for a moment as she warmed back up. She'd let him see the real her this week. She'd let him because she hadn't seen the danger in it. And now he'd seen her, faults and all, and he still wanted her. The unbelievable draw of that began to lure her in, and her breath hitched. "This isn't a nice joke."

"It's not a joke at all. I know what's eating you."

"Do you? Do you really?"

"You think you have to keep everything fun and light. You think you have to fight all emotional ties because they bind, they restrict. But I don't want to hold you back or tell you what you should and shouldn't do. You're a grown woman, a beautiful, smart, incredible woman, and I want you just the way you are."

"Why?"

He blinked. "Why?"

"You've told me yourself you don't do deep relationships. After raising your siblings and then doing the sort of work you do, having someone want you on a daily basis is too much like a burden."

"I didn't say that," he said. "I never called love a burden."

"It was implied."

"Okay, I'll agree, it can be, if it's done one-sided. I've seen too much of that, Lily. Too many of my close friends burned because of unrealistic expectations. But that's not what I'm interested in here. I want a strong, independent woman who has her own goals and dreams, ones that don't depend on mine but can mesh with them."

"My life wouldn't mesh with anyone's."

"It would if you wanted it to."

And wasn't that just the crux. Her heart was beating hard and unnaturally heavy. "I've never wanted it to."

"Me, either. Before you."

Oh, God. The oddest feeling came over her, as if someone was dangling this big, fat, beautiful carrot in front of her, close enough to reach.

But what if it was poisonous? What if it grew teeth and bit her?

Then he capped her panic. "I think I'm falling in love with you, Lily."

Her mouth fell open. But it was the oddest thing, she still couldn't breathe.

"I wasn't looking for you, but it doesn't seem to matter. I found you."

Her throat burned and she shook her head, trying one last time to reason with him. "Easy words."

"You think so?" His eyes glittered with temper now. "You think they're just flying out of my mouth?"

"Okay, maybe *easy* was the wrong word. *Dangerous.*"

"No, my job is dangerous. Your job is dangerous. That's just a fact. What I'm feeling for you has nothing to do with any of that. You can't die from it."

Then why did her heart ache so badly she felt as though she was going to?

"Look, Lily, I came here feeling restless. Like maybe I was floundering a bit, but I didn't know why. I know now."

He was killing her slowly. Torturously. Doing exactly what he'd said he wouldn't. She covered her face with her hands. He was hurting her. "It's only been six nights. Seven days." And a thousand memories.

"Long enough. Something was missing in me before. The most important part. The heart. You, Lily. You were missing."

"I don't want this responsibility." She had too much already.

"My feelings aren't your responsibility, and you know it. Stop finding excuses."

She dropped her hands from her face. "What happened? Why couldn't we keep it light and easy and fun like we wanted?"

He lifted a shoulder. A guy's response.

"This is asinine."

"Not exactly the reaction I was going for."

"I know that," she said to his grim face. "I'm sorry. Give me a minute, my heart is in my throat."

But before she got her minute, her radio squawked.

Sara's voice filled the compartment. "Lily. Oh, my God, Lily. Matt's missing."

"What?"

There were panicked tears in Sara's voice. "He and Debbie went out on snowmobiles. Debbie came back for lunch, thinking Matt was right behind her, but he didn't show up. No one's seen him, and he's not answering his radio."

"We'll be right there." Lily shoved the cat into gear for the short journey to the lodge entrance, not realizing until she put her foot on the accelerator that she'd automatically united her and Logan as a unit by saying "we."

15

LILY COULD HARDLY DRIVE THE Sno-Cat, and it had nothing to do with the fact that more snow had fallen in a single twelve-hour period then she'd ever seen, or that it was still snowing.

It had everything to do with a few little, harmless words that when strung together equaled terror. Logan thought he was falling in love with her. *Love*. The weight of that felt too heavy, far too heavy a load for her to carry.

The snow was coming down harder now and Matt was out there in it. She figured Sara was overreacting as usual, that he could be back already, but she searched the area for him anyway, as she drove toward the front of the lodge. She glanced over at Logan. Did he really almost love her? She couldn't stop the words from repeating themselves in her head, or the low but thoroughly riveting tone in his voice when he'd said them.

Utter confidence. Complete belief.

Her heart hadn't stopped pounding since. What if she was falling, too? She couldn't think of anything worse because love would ruin everything. No matter what he'd promised, there'd be expectations, frustration. Hurt.

As she pulled up to the front of the lodge, Sara raced down the stone steps toward her. Only a narrow strip had been shoveled, and Lily nearly swallowed her heart at how quickly and carelessly Sara moved on the slick path, without a coat or a hat, or even the right boots. Lily hopped out and jammed her own beanie on her sister's head. "Are you crazy?" She wrapped her nice and toasty jacket around Sara, as well. "And you call *me* irresponsible."

"He's hurt, I just know it."

"Okay, take it easy. Who did Debbie leave him up there with?"

"Himself." This from Debbie as she came down the steps. Unlike Sara, she was dressed for the weather, but her eyes, usually cool and sardonic, were filled with worry.

"Damn it," Lily said. "It's against the rules to be up there alone."

"Since when do you care about the rules?" Sara cried. "Just find him."

The words felt like a hard one-two punch to the stomach. *Since when do you care about the rules?* How many damn years had she been respectable, responsible, and still, *still* she got no credit for it? She'd brood over that good and hard, but it would have to be later, when Matt was back safe and sound, when Logan was out of her heart and she was alone to lick her wounds in private.

Sara covered her own face. "I'm sorry. I didn't mean that."

"Forget it."

"No, I won't. I can't. I'm just so damn scared."
Reaching out, she hugged Lily hard. "I know you've
changed. I know it drives you crazy when we treat
you like a baby. I do it all the time, and yet here I am
asking you to save my life."

"Matt's."

"He is my life." A sob escaped her and Lily felt her
heart crack.

"We'll find him."

"I love him ridiculously, Lily. Just like I love you. Go
save my foolish husband for me. Like only you can."

"Tell me what you know," Lily said to Debbie.

"I wanted to ride before I left," Debbie said. "No
one else could take me out, you were all busy."

"Working," Lily said. "You might want to try it
sometime."

Debbie stared at her, then nodded in silent ac-
knowledgement of the barb hitting home. "He took
me to the top. He wanted to go down Sunrise Row
to see how great the powder skiing would be for tomorrow, or whenever you got the lifts going again.
But he didn't come back."

"And now I can't get him on the radio." Sara's
teeth were chattering. "What are we going to do?"

"You're going to go back inside," Lily said. "I'm
going up there to go look for him. Get on the radio
and pull staff in from snow removal to get on the
search, as well. Tell them what you told me about
where he was last seen, and that he was solo." She
glared at Debbie, who shocked her by looking so
miserable that Lily didn't say what was on her mind
but instead turned away.

Debbie grabbed her wrist. "Tell me you can find him."

"I can find him."

"I'm sorry, Lily."

"Just go get warm."

Lily wasn't surprised when Logan followed her to the garage and got on a snowmobile next to her. He slid his helmet on and smiled grimly. "Looks like it's still an *us* thing."

"Looks that way." She started her snowmobile and thought, *And it feels good. Scary good.*

So much to think about. Too much for now. The snow was like a thick, blinding curtain that she wished she could shove out of her way. Their window between snowfalls had turned out to be much shorter than expected. It was late afternoon now, not that she could tell given how dull the daylight was. White, white, white everywhere, and depth perception was long gone. But she knew this mountain like the back of her hand, and took the first hill, pausing at the top.

"There!" Logan had to shout over the roar of the engines when he stopped next to her. "See those faint tracks?"

"The snowfall is taking them out."

"We'll have to hurry," he agreed.

They climbed the next hill, higher now. With the lifts still and nobody around, things seemed strangely alien. Lily looked around, and at the lack of any tracks or sign of Matt, at the snow falling, *dumping*, she felt a building frustration, and a fear. Debbie had turned around here—they could just make out her tracks going back down.

So where was Matt? He knew how hormonal Sara was, and even befuddled by those hormones, he always catered to her feelings and respected them.

That he hadn't been in touch was a bad sign. "Okay, down Sunrise Row. Debbie said that was his plan. He's not big on plans, but maybe this time he stuck to his."

"Wait." Logan reached out and grabbed her arm when she would have gone on. "There. See? I think he went up higher here, not down."

She studied the ground and saw what she'd missed. Sunken tracks nearly completely hidden by fresh snowfall to their left, a trail that would have taken Matt around and up the next hill.

"Come on." Logan let go of her arm and steered his snowmobile after the tracks. It was tough going with so much powder. The snowmobiles were forced to work extra hard, and it took all Lily's concentration not to get stuck. At the top of the next hill, the highest accessible point of the mountain, there were indeed faint tracks.

The incline was sharp and slippery here. Dangerous. If they stayed on one of the high drifts, they could get bogged down in all the powder and end up stuck, something Lily knew from experience could take forever to dig out of. But if they stayed on the sides where the snow hadn't stuck to the packed ice, they faced a slide.

By mutual consent, they risked the drifts. After a few moments, they came close to a jutting peak, not too far from where they'd rescued Pete. Logan gestured to Lily to stay back, then veered toward it himself. "Logan, no!"

But he was gone.

"Damn it." She leaped off her snowmobile and sank into snow nearly up to her thighs. Swearing, she climbed back on and took it as close to the edge as she dared, sagging with relief when she saw Logan still on his snowmobile, about fifteen feet ahead and down the lip of the face. Only feet from the sharp drop-off. "Logan, careful!"

He couldn't possibly hear her over the roar of the engines and the helmet on his head. Heart in her throat, she went after him, praying the snowmobiles held their traction.

Ahead of her, Logan slowed his, then came to a stop. Leaping off, he sank into the snow.

She hopped off, too, practically had to swim through the thick powder toward him.

"He drove along the ridge far ahead," he said. "See?"

"But that's suicide."

"It is to you, because you know the terrain and you know how unstable and dangerous the snow and ice are. But Matt isn't a ski patroller. He's not out here every day. He doesn't know."

But you do, she thought. He'd make it his business to know such things. Looking at him, his long tough body crouched low in the snow, his eyes intent and sharp on the terrain around them as he tracked a man he didn't really know and by rights shouldn't have cared about, an emotion came over her, strong and hot. Uncontainable.

He glanced over at her, and misunderstanding the expression on her face, he shoved up the face guard on his helmet and reached for her hand. "We'll find him, Lily."

At her hip, her walkie-talkie squawked. It was Sara. Chris had set up crews, they were coming up, fanning out. And was there any sign of her husband?

Lily promised her they were close, that they thought they'd found his tracks, and as she said it she silently hoped to God she was telling the truth.

They got back on their snowmobiles and continued to move across the treacherous lip of the cliff, slowly now, not wanting to miss anything. The trees were thick here, with high drifts of snow between them. More was coming down at a shocking rate. She was cold, afraid, shaken, hating that they were searching for Matt, that he could be injured or worse. But there was no denying it—she'd missed this, missed being out here, and she envied Logan for being able to do this every day if necessary. *This* is what she'd been born to do. She had the skills and experience, needed to be out here where she belonged.

Inheriting the resort had been a shock, and she was grateful to her grandma for giving her the experience, the chance to learn the ropes inside and out and to deal with the responsibility, but…and this was a big but…she knew now it wasn't for her.

This was for her.

Impossibly, the snow fell harder, in huge, silent flakes, and the urgency doubled. They had to hurry before there were no tracks to follow at all. Maintaining control took everything Lily had, and she kept glancing at Logan to make sure he was okay, which he definitely was. She supposed years in a helicop-

ter in all sorts of dangerous situations had taught
him to be prepared for anything.

Still, if they found Matt here, injured, she had no
idea how they would be able to extricate him, not in
this weather on this sharp precipice. They were nearly
at a crawl now, and then they stopped altogether.

Though Logan was only a few feet from her, the
blinding snow made him invisible to her. Then his
hand reached through the driving snow and grabbed
hers. "Lily."

She knew what he was going to say and shook her
head. "No."

"The tracks go over."

It was true. The tracks went right over the rise, a
slope so steep that it should have been impossible to
ride. They got off their snowmobiles, Lily's terror a
huge lump in her throat. Logan took her hand,
squeezed it as they made their way as close to the
edge as possible. When they saw the tracks, heading
straight down, disappearing into a grove of snow-
covered trees, she nearly sank to her knees. "Oh, my
God." She reached for her walkie-talkie and called
base, giving them their location, then together they
slid down the slope, her worst fears coming true
when they found a crumpled snowmobile at the base
of a wide pine.

With no sign of Matt.

Lily's stomach plummeted, and they immediately
started combing the area, calling for him. "Matt!"
Her voice bounced off the trees and came back at
her. "*Matt!*"

"Here."

At the weak return cry, she and Logan whipped around. Ahead about ten yards farther down, a white lump leaned back against a tree.

Matt, covered in the fresh snow.

Lily slid down the hill toward him, with Logan right with her. As she got closer, she could see an alarming amount of red mixed in with the snow. Blood. Hers ran cold. *"Logan."*

"I see him. Come on, Lily, let's do what we do." *Let's do what we do.*

His words brought her calm. Strength. And because of him, she had skilled hands and a cool head when she reached for a bleeding and broken Matt.

16

"BREATHING'S SHALLOW," LOGAN said quietly to Lily. They were on either side of Matt, boots braced against the tree so as not to slip down the vertical slope. Lily was carefully trying to free Matt of the snow covering him to see his injuries.

Logan had no idea how long Matt had been down, but given the amount accumulated on him, it'd been at least an hour.

"Oh, Matt." Lily tugged off her gloves and put a bare hand to his frozen face.

"Don't move me."

Shocky but at least coherent, Logan thought, meeting Lily's gaze over his, fear and worry in her eyes. He ran his hands over Matt's limbs, but his dread only increased as he discovered why Matt didn't want to be moved. Looked like a possible fractured femur, some cracked ribs and a nice gash above his eyebrow, which was where the blood had come from.

Lily took in the injuries for herself and had to visibly harden herself. "We won't move you until we have to."

"Just fly me out of here," Matt said.

Again she looked at Logan. They both knew there

was no way they'd get a helicopter in here with all these trees, and even if they could, the weather was too far gone for that.

They had no choice but to get him down the hill first. "Matt," Lily said.

Matt closed his eyes. "I really screwed this up."

Logan had already taken off his jacket and wrapped it around Matt's torso, and Lily removed hers, as well, setting it over his legs, trying to keep him safe from hypothermia. "Look at it this way," she said. "You're already injured so Sara can't do much worse to you for vanishing on her. Where the hell is your radio?"

"Lost it."

Logan slid his fingers against Matt's wrist to take his pulse. Weak and thready. He shook his head at Lily.

She removed her helmet and reached for her radio with a shaking hand. It wasn't the first time Logan had seen her remain cool and calm under incredible pressure, but it was the first time he'd seen it cost her. He wanted to make this okay for her, but he couldn't, and knowing she was strong enough to deal with it, knowing in fact that he could count on her to be just as strong as he was, was an amazing thing.

She was amazing. He'd never been with a woman like her before, one just as capable and resilient as anyone on his SAR team. What would it be like to be with her day in and day out, knowing his back was covered through thick and thin?

"I'm going to make it?" Matt's voice shook as his body trembled violently. "Right?"

"Well, I'm sure as hell not dealing with a pregnant Sara alone," Lily said, trying to be tough and failing.

Matt didn't notice. "The baby," he said softly, and a dreamy smile covered his face. "I almost forgot…"

"Don't tell Sara that."

He frowned. "Head hurts."

"Yeah, you cracked it good." She eyed the line of blood that had oozed from the wound, drying now.

"Stay awake," Logan said when Matt's lids dropped.

"Don't want to."

"Too bad." Lily leaned in so she was nose to nose with him. "Don't you go to sleep. Don't you dare."

"Hm-mmm."

"Matthew Edward Wallace." Her voice shook now as she grabbed his jacket. "Don't you leave me. Don't you leave Sara. Or that baby. *Matt!*"

"Yeah. Here." Matt winced. "Just…resting my damn eyes." He licked his dry lips. "Don't you guys have chocolate or something? Aren't you rescue people supposed to offer me chocolate?"

Lily sat back and let out a low laugh, squeezing Logan's hand when he reached for hers. He looked into her eyes and saw her fear for Matt, her uncertainty that they could actually get him down without doing more harm. He squeezed her hand again and for one brief moment, she clung.

From her, the gesture felt like a shouted declaration of her feelings, and it jerked his own to the surface. But he heard snowmobile engines in the distance. Letting go of her, he scrambled up the hill to flag the other rescuers down, a feat in itself in the deep, thick snow.

The snowmobiles had to be left at the top of the

cliff. It took a series of people and ski poles used as stakes on the vertical climb in order to get ready to move Matt. His condition had deteriorated and he kept shifting in and out of consciousness. They got him in a litter with a cervical collar around his neck and a hard board beneath his back, but a smooth lift wasn't possible with the steep, unforgiving terrain. Twice the litter slipped a few feet, once setting off a slide of snow.

Lily held her breath the entire time, watching the hill carefully because they were ripe for an avalanche, which would just top this whole disaster off nicely. But a nerve-racking forty-five minutes later, he was up at the top, the litter attached to a snowmobile.

Getting him down took a coordinated effort of the snowmobiles. Two in front to try to make a steady track, a difficult enough task with the steadily falling snow that had covered their route already. Following them went the snowmobile that towed Matt, and then another behind, on the radio, calling out the condition of the litter and whether it was a steady enough ride for their patient.

As the procession took off, Lily turned to Logan. She felt overwhelmed with emotion.

"It's only been a week," she said.

He didn't blink at the ridiculous and quick subject change. He didn't scoff it off or laugh. He just nodded, and she could have loved him for that alone. "The best week of my life."

"It's not long enough to know," she whispered, and shoved up her face guard.

"Some things don't take a lot of time." He stroked

a gloved hand over her jaw. "You're one of those things for me."

She shook her head, even as she grabbed his hand and held it to her face. "I'm not ready for you to go."

"Then come with me. Come to my world for a week. For longer. For whatever you can give me."

Go to his world... He could have no idea how tempting that was. She didn't understand what it was inside her that made her fight this thing so hard when in truth, she wanted him so very much. The depth of his concern and compassion, coupled with what he'd claimed to feel for her and what she saw in his eyes, robbed her of speech. He was so solid, so right, so good for her, and she buried her hands in his jacket, tugging him close, kissing him hard. He instantly reciprocated, gliding his arms around her and hauling her close with a low groan that reached in and wrapped around her heart.

He loved her.

Loved her.

Staggering, really. But somewhere along the way, the hard knot of panic had loosened—slightly, anyway—and just thinking it began a glow of warmth from the inside out.

Only a couple of hours passed from the time they'd set out looking for him until they made it back to the lodge, but in that time, the storm had worsened and the roads were all closed again. Logan wasn't going anywhere for a while, but worse, neither was Matt.

They got him inside the first-aid room. Because the lifts had never opened, there wasn't a medic on duty, but Lily, Logan, and Chris all had medical training. They stayed in touch with the local E.R. by phone, doing what they could for Matt, making sure he was warm and stayed still. Sara made sure he stayed awake.

She could have kept the dead awake the way she wailed at the sight of her husband. Lily tried to calm her down, but nothing could do that. Even Matt wanted the hell out and kept asking if the roads were clear. Logan wanted desperately for Matt to be able to get out and get to the hospital.

But for himself, he'd have been fine if the snowstorm never let up.

LILY GRABBED A BADLY NEEDED moment alone, standing just outside the first-aid room, protected from the snow by the roof's overhang, staring out into the storm.

Footsteps came up behind her, and then Aunt Debbie appeared at her side. "I need a moment with you."

Lily glanced at her, all decked out in her usual expensive finery. The only thing missing was her mocking smile. "Sorry. I'm exhausted and not up for any witty repartee."

"You put your life on the line to save Matt. You did it without even blinking."

Lily lifted a shoulder. "I blinked plenty."

"You do that every day," Debbie said softly in an awed voice that had Lily taking another look at her.

Wow. Aunt Debbie was really impressed by her. Stop the presses. "Have you somehow missed the meaning of *ski patrol*, and the fact that I've been on it for years?"

"Yes," Debbie said honestly. "I have. And I want

to tell you in advance that I'm sorry, though I don't deserve for you to accept my apology."

"What are you talking about?"

"When Mom left you this place, I was green with envy."

"You were not. You said good riddance and moved to New York."

"No, I believe my exact words to you were that I wished I believed in voodoo so I could curse you with pins and needles and watch you die a slow, torturous death."

Lily laughed.

Debbie's lips quirked. "Yeah, you did that then, too. And since most of what I wanted to do to you is frowned on in today's society, I settled for talking bad about you every chance I could." Her smile faded. "And playing silly little pranks on you to amuse myself."

A chill took hold of Lily that had nothing to do with the storm outside. "What?"

"Like removing a few out-of-bounds signs, screwing with your food deliveries, putting up party posters, messing with your computers. Even tossing random files from your desk into the trash."

Lily stared at her. "And then today with Matt…?"

"No! God, no, I didn't get him hurt on purpose." Debbie's eyes filled. "That was just stupid, dumb, bad luck."

Lily saw the tortured honesty in her aunt's eyes, and swearing lavishly, she paced the deck. This was unbelievable. She'd been racking her brain, trying to figure out if one of her staff members, or even a guest, could have been the one causing trouble, and all along it had been the one person she'd never even considered. Sure, Aunt Debbie had been a pain in the ass, with her demands and her the-world-owes-me-service attitude, but this…this betrayal was way over the top.

"You did hear the *I'm sorry* part, right?" Debbie asked her when she came close again.

"Why the hell would you do any of this?"

"I told you. I was jealous. Here we were, two peas in a wild pod, and yet somehow you still managed to make my mother believe you could handle all this."

"I didn't ask for it."

"No, that only made it worse." Debbie's smile was sad now. "Because you pulled it off in spite of not wanting to. I wanted to hate you for that, and instead I only love you more. Damn it. Now if you want to kick me out, I get it. But I'm telling you I'm done making trouble for you."

Lily could only let out a baffled laugh. "Do you want me to thank you? Do you know how many times you sicced Gwyneth and Sara on me, making my life a living hell?"

"Yeah." Debbie sighed in remembered pleasure. "And that was always fun to watch. I wish my sister and I were as close as you three."

"You are insane. We're not close."

"Aren't you?"

Lily looked out into the storm as her thoughts raced. Gwyneth was a sanctimonious pain in her ass, but she always had Lily's back, always, whether Lily wanted her to or not. And so did Sara.

And she had theirs.

"I'll leave as soon as I can get out," Debbie said. "I think I might have overstayed my welcome this time."

"What, you think you can just create havoc all over the lodge, and then disappear to leave someone else to clean up your mess?"

"I can't believe you'd want me to stay."

"I don't want you to stay. I don't want you anywhere near me right now. But you're going to face the consequences of your selfishness, and you're going to do it here. When this crisis is all over, when Matt's safely in the hospital and the guests are home, you're going to sit down with Gwyneth and Sara and you're going to explain exactly what you did to me, to the lodge, and why. It will be up to us as a family to decide where we go from there. Until then, you are going to stay in the lodge and you are going to work your ass off. Cleaning rooms, bussing tables in the cafeteria, shoveling snow— Whatever this lodge needs, you're going to do it."

There was a split second when she thought Debbie was going to argue, was going to come back with a smart-ass comment, but then she straightened her shoulders and met Lily's gaze. "If you're willing to have me here, then fine. I suppose it's the least I can do."

"Damn right it is," Lily said, trying to stop her hands from shaking in the aftermath of way too much adrenaline flooding through her system. She'd take a mountain cliff in a storm any day over this kind of crap. "You can start now, by washing down the tables in the cafeteria."

Debbie simply nodded. And then she was gone, leaving Lily alone, watching the snow fall in eerie silence, wondering why everything seemed… wrong.

LILY HAD NEVER KNOWN THE SNOW to fall so relentlessly. It continued to come down at the rate of a foot an hour, choking the life right out of the entire Tahoe basin and seeming to put her entire world into a weird time freeze, where everything that was wrong stood in ultraclear focus.

"At least we have food," Matt muttered, half delirious, half wasted with pain meds. "We're not going to have to turn into the Donner party." He forced his eyes open. "Promise me we're not going to turn into the Donner party. The weak got eaten first, and I'm feeling pretty damn weak at the moment."

Sara stroked his hair. "I promise to eat Gwyneth and Lily first."

"Okay, then." He smiled faintly, and Sara just sat there staring at him as if she could heal him if she wished for it hard enough. Lily could hardly bear to watch her sister's anguish.

As dark fell and more hours passed, Gwyneth pulled Lily aside in the first-aid room. Lily tried to hold on to what was left of her patience

She had her hands full worrying about Matt, the trapped guests and a distraught Sara, who kept throwing her arms around Lily, saying she was the most incredible sister ever. That was just new enough to have Lily liking it. "What?"

"I wanted to talk to you," Gwyneth whispered.

"I know things are all messed up, but you can yell at me later."

Gwyneth's mouth dropped open. "You think I want to yell at you for all that's gone wrong today?"

"Don't you?" Lily looked over Gwyneth's shoulder to Logan, who was bending over Matt, talking to him, trying to keep his spirits up, though Matt's leg and ribs were costing him considerable pain. Lily worried about how badly he needed surgery, about the possibility of internal injuries that they couldn't diagnose without an E.R. Her heart squeezed, hard.

"The radio says that the snow will be letting up in a few more hours. When it does, we'll kick everything into gear. We'll get Matt to a hospital, the guests in and out…and Logan to the airport." The reference to Logan seemed to slip out accidentally, reminding her of his words.

Come to my world, he'd said, probably never dreaming she'd actually consider it. And then, as if he felt her eyes on him, he straightened and looked right at her, with everything he'd claimed to feel for her in his eyes.

To take or leave.

"Oh, Lily." Gwyneth, queen bee, tyrant and a half, ruler of both her universe and Lily's, stood there as her eyes filled. "You feel for him," she whispered. "It's beautiful."

"No, it's not. It's…messy."

Gwyneth laughed even as a tear fell.

Unease filled Lily's belly. "What are you doing?"

"Trying to tell you something."

"What? And why are you crying?"

"What you do around here couldn't be done by

anyone else, including me. I think I'm finally getting that. You have strength and commitment in spades and I'm sorry I ever let you feel like you didn't. Lily, I think you're incredible." Gwyneth hugged her hard. "Incredible," she repeated softly, and walked away.

Lily could only stare after her. Both her sisters thought she was the best thing since sliced bread today, which felt odd for a couple of reasons. One, she was the same person she'd been yesterday, last week. Even last year. Nothing had changed, so to be so suddenly accepted made her feel...off balance.

She'd finally proven herself to them, and yet the strangest thing was that she'd discovered she no longer needed their approval. She was okay with herself, she liked herself, and though it was lovely to have her family on board with her, their acceptance didn't change anything. "Gwyneth?"

Her sister stopped and turned. "Yeah?"

"If Grandma had died this week instead of last year, and left you the resort now, what would you do?"

Gwyneth smiled. "Do you trust me, Lily? I mean really trust me?"

"I haven't," she said honestly.

"I know. But now?"

Lily cocked her head, surprised by all she saw in her sister's eyes. "I think maybe I do."

Gwyneth just smiled and walked away.

What did that mean? She looked over at Matt in bed. Logan sat at his side, reading from a joke book someone had hunted up. Sara sat on his other side. Every minute or so, Matt patted her arm, reassuring her he was alive. Lily watched the wordless glances they shared, glances that expressed everything they felt with such ease.

Because it unnerved her, made her feel things she wasn't ready to feel, she left the room and tried to bury herself in work. There was certainly enough to do, but everywhere she turned, what had to be done was being done. Logan had Matt's care covered, Gwyneth had managed any business stuff, the cafeteria was still up and running and Chris was handling snow-removal crews.

But damn it, she stood outside her office needing something to do so she could turn her damn mind off.

"Hey," Logan said, and tugged her around to face him. "It's late. Why don't you sleep?"

"I don't want to be asleep if Matt needs me."

"He's got plenty of care. Chris came in to be with him for a while."

"But—"

"The snow's still coming down, but the radar confirms a letup coming in a few hours," he said. "I double-checked with the hospital. They're sending an ambulance for Matt soon as the roads clear."

The long, tenuous rescue came back to her—witnessing Matt's incredible pain, knowing that if he'd been out there any longer they might have lost him. And just like that, she broke. "Oh, God."

He opened his arms, bringing them hard around her. "Hey, he's going to be okay. He's going to be in a helluva lot of pain for a while, but he's going to be okay."

She nodded and let herself cling, pressing her face

to his throat, inhaling the innate scent of him that she'd grown so attached to in just a matter of days. In only one more, he'd be gone. He'd already be gone if Mother Nature hadn't intervened. She tightened her arms.

He let out a low sound and held on. "You never changed your clothes after the rescue."

"I'm okay."

"You've got to be chilled. Come on, let's go get you warm. Maybe get some sleep, too. Sara and Gwyneth have everything under control." Before she could protest, he'd led her to her room, nudged her inside and toward the bathroom for a hot shower.

She had to admit the hot water on her sore, chilled body felt incredible, but something was missing. Someone. She slid open the curtain to call out for Logan, but he was right there, waiting with dark, melting eyes. "In," she said, and tugged him into the shower, clothes and all.

Laughing softly, he hauled her close and kissed her, long and slow. She had no idea how he could make her feel so cherished and yet so hot and itchy at the same time, but he did. He always did. Together they stripped him out of his clothes, but when she tried to wrap her legs around him to draw him inside her body, he shook his head. "In the bed," he said softly against her mouth.

But her body was already humming, throbbing and halfway to bliss because of that shocking way he had of getting her to come with seemingly no effort. "Logan—"

"*Bed.*" And he lifted her himself, dropping her, wet and still steaming, to the mattress, following her down.

17

SHE SHOULDN'T WANT HIM NOW, Lily thought, even as her breath hitched and she opened her arms, welcoming Logan's weight. Not like this, as if she needed him more than life itself. She shouldn't be able to lose herself in him with so much on her mind, but she could. She did.

She was afraid she always would.

The night was a dark one, with no moon and only the glow of the steadily falling snow slanting in the window and over the bed like a pale night-light. Just enough to see his face, taut with desire for her. His eyes, dark and deep, his firm mouth curved as it met hers.

Her blood stirred, as it always did with him, and with it came a low, throbbing need she'd never experienced with anyone else, making her heart beat with a heavy anticipation.

Gliding his fingers in her hair, his thumbs tilted her jaw up so that he could study her face. "Lily," he said, and then took her mouth, coaxing it open with warm lips and a hot tongue that danced to hers in a way that made her melt.

He always made her melt, just by looking at her, just by being. His hands slid up and down her back as he continued to kiss her, slow and deep, his fingers skimming down her hips, cupping her bottom, squeezing gently as his mouth made its way down her throat, over her collarbone, licking and nibbling and tasting as he went. He drew her breast into his mouth as his hand dipped between her thighs, making her ache with an easy touch that seemed even more intense and arousing every time.

Repetition had always bored her, but nothing about Logan came even close. In fact, his familiarity with her body only made it all the more exciting, and it built within her, layer over layer of heat and affection in the dark, cold night.

Even when she gasped out his name and dug her nails into his flesh as she began to shudder, he kept at her, leisurely and steadily, achingly so.

He wasn't unaffected. His skin was damp and heated, his heart pounded fiercely against hers. His breath caught when she returned the favor and skimmed her hands over every inch of him. When she replaced her fingers with her tongue, it tore a rough groan from him, and when she took him too close to the edge, he pulled free. Tumbling her to her back on the mattress, he held her busy hands at her sides, nuzzling his way past her belly button, between her thighs. He brought her to a peak with his mouth, his moan mixing with hers as she shuddered in ecstasy for long, lost moments. "Again," he whispered against her wet, hot flesh.

Arching, every pulse point pounding, she reached for him, needing more than anything for him to sink into her, mate with her, needing to give herself over to him and have him do the same. She wanted to see it, to watch his face as he did, the hunger so vivid and real, her throat burned, her eyes filled.

When he finally lifted her hips and slid into her, she felt her heart give, and as she let him in, a tear slid down her cheek, sweet and sorrowful at the same time. *The last time*, she thought. This was the last time for him to hold her, touch her… She couldn't even think it, so she pushed it out of her head and rocked to him, breathing his name as he breathed hers. He thrust in deeply as he kissed her, giving her his body, his heart and soul. Love for her flickered in his dark eyes, and her own heart and soul stumbled.

And fell.

And still she watched him love her, watched as the pleasure crossed his face, watched as he let himself go, holding nothing back.

And then fell all the more for it.

LILY WOKE UP SLOWLY, A LITTLE groggily. Turning her head, she caught a glimpse of the clock. Four in the morning. She'd slept for only an hour.

She lay entwined with Logan, her hand on his chest, absorbing his slow, deep breathing while she stared at the ceiling in the dark. Sex had always been a fun way to pass the time. But with Logan, it was so far beyond fun, she couldn't even define it. And even she, a virgin in the love department, knew this hadn't been just sex.

No, they'd made love, slow and sweet and hot and unbearably heart-and-soul-wrenching. It was too much, too fast. Any sane person would agree.

Some big risk taker she'd turned out to be. But the truth was, hanging off a cliff had never been as hard as this.

Nothing had. She felt panicked, with none of her usual peace and strength anywhere to be found.

Over the past years, she'd believed Bay Moon had provided that peace and strength. But for the first time she understood it wasn't the mountain supplying them at all. No, they'd come from within her.

Only they were both missing now. She slipped out of the bed and, in the dark, let herself take one last glimpse of the man who'd changed her life just by being in it for a week. Then she turned away, dressed and slipped out of the room.

The lodge was quiet, a good thing at this hour. On her way to check on Matt, she stopped in her office and checked the weather radar. The snow had just let up, but the break would last only until midday. She checked for messages. The ambulance was on its way. Chris had the crews out clearing the lot.

People would have to work fast to get on and off the mountain today. Including Logan.

She'd already gotten more time with him than expected, she reminded herself. Last night had been a bonus. She'd never forget it.

She made her way toward First Aid. Matt was flat on his back, his leg immobilized, the IV the hospital had asked for hanging above him. He was fast asleep. Sara lay beside him, carefully draped over his good side, also asleep. They had their faces nuzzled close to each other.

They were so in love it hurt to look at them. How

had Sara done it, let herself fall? And why hadn't she faced any of the panic that Lily faced? What made it so easy for some?

And so hard for her?

In his sleep, Matt groaned, a sound of pain, and Sara immediately cupped his face, stroking him gently until he settled in again. Lily knew Sara would do anything for Matt, including taking his pain on herself if she could.

Her heart squeezed. She'd do the same for Logan, and the thought made her feel raw and open, too much so. Vulnerable. God, she couldn't take it. Her heart hurt, her vision blurred—

A hand settled on her shoulder and she nearly jerked out of her skin. Whipping around, she came face-to-face with Logan. "You scared me," she whispered, putting a hand to her bruised heart.

His eyes locked on hers. He reached out and stroked away the tear she hadn't even realized she'd let fall. "What is it?"

What was it? She had no idea where to start, and she was afraid that if she tried, she'd fall apart. "I don't know."

"Yes, you do." He turned her to face where Matt and Sara lay, entangled together as if they'd been made for each other. One so hurt, the other lending their strength and support and love. "You know exactly," he said softly in her ear. "You're looking at them, yearning for what they have. Why the hell can't you admit it?"

Straightening away from him, she swiped at her tears and crossed her arms over her chest. Closing herself off.

But he just looked at her, patience shining in his eyes.

Ah, hell. Why lie? "Fine," she admitted. "I'm looking at them, yearning for what they have. *Happy?*"

Wrapping a hand around her wrist, he dragged her out of the doorway and just around the corner, pressing her back against the wall as he touched her face. "If there's something you want, Lily, just take it."

Another tear fell. Damn it. The *last*. "How? How do I even really know it's there for the taking?"

"You have to believe." He shot her a half smile. "I'll even make you a deal. I'll take the first risk...." He picked up the hand lying limp at her side, pressing it to his heart. "Remember when I said I thought I was falling in love with you?"

"I'm not likely to forget."

"Well, I'm not just thinking it anymore. I know." He tightened his fingers on her when she would have pulled away. "I'm in love with you, Lily." He offered her a shaky smile. "I know I promised no strings attached, and I still mean that. I don't want to hold you back. I wouldn't." He drew in a long, shaky breath. "So. How's that for risk?"

She couldn't smile back, she was frozen to the spot, every muscle tense. "Pretty good."

"We understand each other. I think it could work."

"But you live in Ohio. I live here in Tahoe."

"I'm flexible. I can come back and forth. And you're restless here, you know it. Come see where I live, come volunteer on the SAR team and get a thrill. Maybe you'll find out you can have more than one home base."

She just stared at him, thinking maybe, just maybe, he could be right.

But he must have taken her silence the wrong way because he gripped her arms and pulled her closer, his eyes flashing with frustration, temper and an emotion so real and unwavering, she could hardly breathe. "I can see backing off because of a fundamental, compelling problem that can't be fixed. Like you hate all men who ski better than you—"

She let out a choking laugh.

"And I can see backing off because you don't ever see yourself falling for me. But goddamn it, don't make excuses, because I'm willing to go wherever it takes, do whatever has to be done to make this work."

She managed to swallow. Not easy with a lump the size of a regulation basketball in her throat. "I can't fall in love after only one week," she said more to herself than anything. "I…can't."

But why not?

If Sara could make a relationship work, if Gwyneth could soften and learn to compromise, then Lily herself could certainly change.

Logan just looked at her, still holding her arms, still in her space, making her body hum and her heart squeeze. "Don't be afraid," he said very quietly. "Not of this."

"Of course not. I'm fearless, remember?"

He let out a low laugh, and pressed his lips to her temple. "Lily."

She gripped him tight, pulling him in for a hug, closing her eyes. Then she opened them and met his. "Okay, listen. I think maybe I— No. Scratch that, start over." She gulped in a big breath and rushed out the words that were threatening to block off her air. "Damn it. I love you back."

He seemed to reel over that, and she let out a long, shaky breath, then laughed at the both of them looking so shell-shocked, more nervous than they'd been while risking life and limb on top of a sheer mountain precipice in a hell of a snowstorm. "I really do, Logan. I love you back."

His eyes were brilliantly shiny. "You didn't melt."

"Are you sure? Because I think the bones dissolved right out of my legs." Feeling rubbery, she slid to the floor.

Logan crouched in front of her. In his eyes was relief, and more love than she'd ever imagined could be staring right back at her. His mouth curved in a smile. "I'm feeling a little shaky myself."

He looked so damn gorgeous, she could hardly stand it. He was hers. Hers. Her shakiness was quickly becoming replaced by an adrenaline surge, and something else...a rush of joy. Wrapping her hands in his shirt, she brought him to her, meeting his mouth with hers for a long, liquidy kiss. When she pulled back, she could feel the gratifying pounding of his heart beneath her palms, and it matched hers perfectly. "We're crazy, you know that," she whispered.

"Undoubtedly."

"This isn't going to be easy."

"Nope."

"Neither of us has a clue how to make something like this work."

"True enough."

"But I want it, so much," she whispered, and threw herself at him so they toppled over on the floor of the hallway. "I want it enough to go with you to Ohio and take some time. Enough to get you to come back here as often as you can."

Flat on his back, he smiled at her, and everything within her softened and went weak and trembly— and strong and sure at the same time. It was right, she thought with awe. It was so right.

From down the hall and on the other side of the big, open lodge came a blip of a siren. Blue and red lights flashed through the darkened resort. The ambulance had arrived. They pulled each other up and she peeked around the corner, into the room where Matt and Sara still lay asleep. From the window came the light pink tinge of dawn. "It's nearly morning," she whispered.

Logan's arm slipped around her waist, pulled her to his side. His lips brushed over her hair. "A new day."

Tilting her head up, she met his mouth with hers. "A new beginning."

Epilogue

Denton, Ohio
Three months later

LOGAN DROVE HOME AFTER A long day of rescues. A surprise spring ice storm had trapped hikers, bikers and motorists alike in situations that had kept his team busy for twenty-two straight hours.

He had two more days of flying ahead of him, and then he was off for four days.

He'd be heading back to Tahoe.

To Lily.

They'd seen each other more often than he'd imagined possible. She loved his small hometown. As a certified EMT, she'd been easily added to their SAR team on a volunteer, on-call basis, and they'd had many adventures over the past few months.

But now it'd been two weeks since he'd seen her. Too long, he thought as he got out of his truck and let himself into his old, renovated farmhouse. Too damn long, and he chafed at the restraints he'd promised her wouldn't be a problem. Ironic, really, since he'd been the one to say that they could make their two lives mesh together, that he'd never put demands on her time or make her choose between his world and hers.

And yet he wanted more, so much more. He stripped out of his clothes and stepped into a steamy shower. When he was done, he pulled on a pair of jeans and stood in front of his opened armoire, staring at the little box he'd put on a shelf there. Flipping it open, he studied the shiny diamond. He ran his thumb over it, wishing it was time to give it away.

At the knock on his door, he put the ring back and headed through his living room to pull open the door. Then stood there in shock.

Lily smiled a little nervously, as if unsure of her welcome. He didn't know how she'd gotten here, or why, and he didn't care. Suddenly everything felt okay in his world. Hauling her over the threshold and into his arms, he kissed her hello. It took a while because it had been two very long weeks and he had a lot of hello in him.

"I love you," she said when he finally lifted his head. "I just couldn't stay away anymore."

"Thank God for that."

"I should tell you right now, I'm no longer in possession of any mountain assets. I gave the controlling portion of the resort to Gwyneth and Sara. They've asked Aunt Debbie to come join them. They're so much better suited to all the day-to-day workings of the thing anyway, and I can come and go now, whenever I want." She hadn't taken a breath, and now pressed a hand to her heart. "I'm rambling, I know, but I just couldn't stand the past two weeks, and I can't always expect you to just drop everything and come to me, especially since I love being here, too, flying with you, working on search and rescue... Did I say I love you?"

Love swamped him. "Don't ever stop saying that to me." He pulled her in and shut the door, then began removing her clothing. "And don't ever start wearing a bra," he added fervently when he wrenched her blouse down her arms and found her gloriously naked beneath.

"I figured I'd probably have to buy a few after I had the kids. Saggage, and all."

He went utterly still and cut his eyes to hers as his world screeched to a stop. "Do you figure they'll be my kids, too?"

"I'm hoping so, seeing as you're so fine to look at."

He couldn't breathe. "So you're going to marry me, then?"

"If you're asking…"

"God. Lily— Hold that thought." Grabbing her hand, he pulled her down the hall to his bedroom.

With a laugh, she glanced at the unmade bed. "Goody."

He pulled her past the bed and ripped open his armoire, grabbed the ring box. Thrust it into her hands.

She stared at it, then lifted her face. "Logan."

"Here." Because he couldn't stand it, he opened it for her. A square-cut diamond in a simple platinum setting winked up at them.

"You…bought this for me?"

"I did."

"But… My God," she whispered, and reverently touched it. "It's beautiful."

"Not as beautiful as you are. Say yes, Lily."

She blinked, but a tear slipped down her cheek anyway. "How about *hell*, *yes*."

He waited until she'd slipped it on her finger to bring her hand up to his mouth, then pressed it against his heart. "I love you."

"I know. I'm getting very fond of hearing that."

"Good." He hauled her up into his arms and twirled her around. "I was looking at the ring just now, before you came, wondering how the hell to get to this." He stroked a hand down her hair and stared into her eyes. "To being an official us."

"Us." She smiled, the amazing, beautiful, strong woman who'd changed his life forever. "I like the sound of that."

"Me, too, Lily. Me, too."

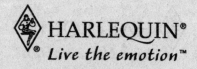

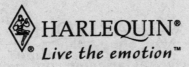

If you enjoyed what you just read,
then we've got an offer you can't resist!

Take 2 bestselling love stories FREE!

Plus get a FREE surprise gift!

Clip this page and mail it to Harlequin Reader Service®

IN U.S.A.	IN CANADA
3010 Walden Ave.	P.O. Box 609
P.O. Box 1867	Fort Erie, Ontario
Buffalo, N.Y. 14240-1867	L2A 5X3

YES! Please send me 2 free Blaze™ novels and my free surprise gift. After receiving them, if I don't wish to receive anymore, I can return the shipping statement marked cancel. If I don't cancel, I will receive 4 brand-new novels each month, before they're available in stores! In the U.S.A., bill me at the bargain price of $3.99 plus 25¢ shipping and handling per book and applicable sales tax, if any*. In Canada, bill me at the bargain price of $4.47 plus 25¢ shipping and handling per book and applicable taxes**. That's the complete price and a savings of at least 10% off the cover prices—what a great deal! I understand that accepting the 2 free books and gift places me under no obligation ever to buy any books. I can always return a shipment and cancel at any time. Even if I never buy another book from Harlequin, the 2 free books and gift are mine to keep forever.

150 HDN DZ9K
350 HDN DZ9L

Name	(PLEASE PRINT)	
Address	Apt.#	
City	State/Prov.	Zip/Postal Code

Not valid to current Harlequin Blaze™ subscribers.

Want to try two free books from another series?
Call 1-800-873-8635 or visit www.morefreebooks.com.

* Terms and prices subject to change without notice. Sales tax applicable in N.Y.
** Canadian residents will be charged applicable provincial taxes and GST.
  All orders subject to approval. Offer limited to one per household.
  ® and ™ are registered trademarks owned and used by the trademark owner and or its licensee.

BLZ04R   ©2004 Harlequin Enterprises Limited.

AMERICAN HEROES

These men are heroes—
strong, fearless...
And impossible to resist!

Join bestselling authors Lori Foster, Donna Kauffman
and Jill Shalvis as they deliver up

MEN OF COURAGE

Harlequin anthology
May 2003

Followed by *American Heroes* miniseries
in Harlequin Temptation

RILEY by Lori Foster
June 2003

SEAN by Donna Kauffman
July 2003

LUKE by Jill Shalvis
August 2003

Don't miss this sexy new miniseries by some of
Temptation's hottest authors!

Available at your favorite retail outlet.

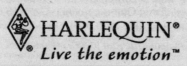

HARLEQUIN®
Live the emotion™

Visit us at www.eHarlequin.com

HTAH

HARLEQUIN® *Blaze*™

Get ready to check in to Hush...

Piper Devon has opened a hot new hotel
that caters to the senses...and it's giving
ex-lover Trace Winslow a few sleepless nights.

Check out

#178 HUSH

by Jo Leigh

Available April 2005

Book #1, Do Not Disturb miniseries

Look for linked stories by Isabel Sharpe,
Alison Kent, Nancy Warren, Debbi Rawlins
and Jill Shalvis in the months to come!

Shhh...Do Not Disturb

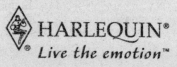

HARLEQUIN®
Live the emotion™